MW01182033

ALSO BY KKUURRTT

Good at Drugs
Blech Life
Give Me A Bad Movie Over A Good One Anyday

ALSO BY TEX GRESHAM

Sunflower
Heck, Texas

Easy Rider II:
Sleazy
Driver(s)

Easy Rider II: Sleazy Driver(s)

by
KKUURRTT & Tex Gresham
or
Tex Gresham & **KKUURRTT**
and
Cavin Bryce Gonzalez
feat.
Brian Alan Ellis
and...

100 & 900%
press

<u>KKUURRTT</u>
What am I supposed to put here?

<u>TEX</u>
This is for Peter, Dennis, and Jack.
And for all the ghosts that have ever haunted me.

"That's what it's all about, all right.
But talkin' about it and bein' it,
that's two different things.
I mean, it's real hard to be free
when you are bought and sold in the marketplace."

"Here's to the first of the day, fellas.
To ol' D. H. Lawrence."

—George Hanson (Jack Nicholson)
Easy Rider (1969)

- PROLOGUE -

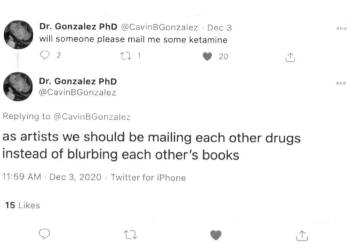

Dr. Gonzalez PhD @CavinBGonzalez · Dec 3
will someone please mail me some ketamine

2   1   20

Dr. Gonzalez PhD
@CavinBGonzalez

Replying to @CavinBGonzalez

as artists we should be mailing each other drugs instead of blurbing each other's books

11:59 AM · Dec 3, 2020 · Twitter for iPhone

15 Likes

KKUURRTT @wwwkurtcom · Dec 3
Replying to @CavinBGonzalez
Uhhh why do Back Patio books cost $72.99?

1   2

Dr. Gonzalez PhD @CavinBGonzalez · Dec 3
lick the pages and find out 💯

2

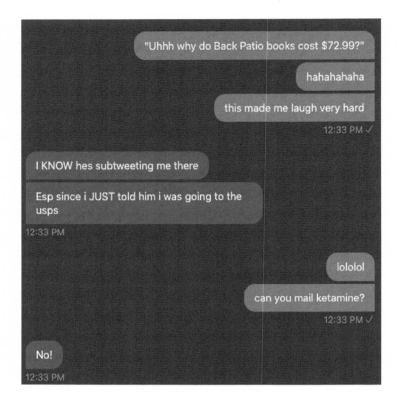

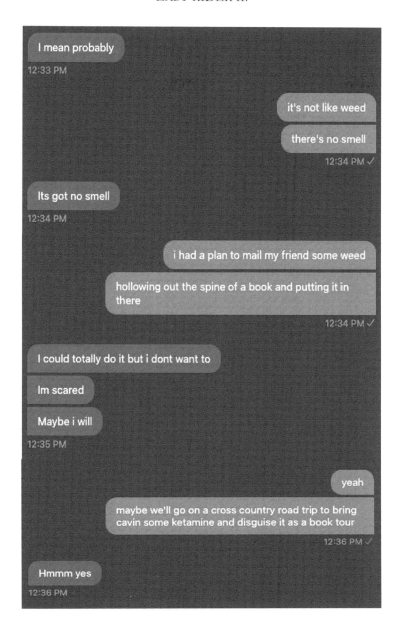

- CALIFORNIA -

KURT

This is a documentary. A film. Released in theatres, yes, but not 3,000, a couple of hundred spread out in cities where the people who make the art that gets released in theatres live. New York and Los Angeles. San Diego and Las Vegas. Orlando fucking Florida. It will go on to get four and a half stars from RogerEbert.com, an internet ghost of the man who once made movies matter to Johnny Jetson and Lisa Public after a successful run of newspaper reviews in the *Chicago Sun Times* and eventually a tv show on PBS with some other guy that changed the way we review movies (with our thumbs). This documentary starts like every auto fictional documentary —with a camera looking at oneself in the bathroom mirror. Insight. Selfie.

The Samsung Galaxy S8 has a 12 megapixel camera that shoots video in 4K so why would anyone need anything else? Sure, Tex is investing in a whole set up—dash mount GoPro, Black Magic, probably that same camera that the main character in *Paranormal Activity* slogs around the entire time, but I'm perfectly satisfied with the one that already lives in my pocket. I have instead invested in a new phone case because the last one was so filled with dust and dirt that all video looked like it was being shot on one of those bright days where the dust mites fly through the sun shine. Really brought the footage down from 4K to maybe 2 or 3.

Okay, got the selfie. I looked foreboding enough with my hoodie hood pulled over my head as if to say this man means business. No external monologue needed, that's a wrap on today cut and print and send it to the editor. Now I need to buy drugs. An action that will undoubtedly not be on camera, but done in private, person to person connection not digitized out to Instagram live putting my girl on blast for just finding the basic economic benefits in sharing what she has access to and most of the rest of us do not. Catch is I don't actually have her number so I have to call LYLE.

LYLE: Yo
KURT: What's up?
LYLE: Nothing just trying to figure out how to get my fucking computer to work.
KURT: What's it doing?
LYLE: Not fucking working.
KURT: Ah, I can call back later.
LYLE: Nah, what's up?
KURT: Oh, uh. Can you holler at [REDACTED] for me? I need some K.

K is Ketamine, but we're gonna skip right over the short hand and pretend that you actually read the DM conversations that preface this documentary fiction and can track your way through basic context clues to an actual understanding of where we're headed here. This is a road trip after all. The great American adventure. Perpetual forward motion or we're basically permanently stagnating. Permanent punctuation. Instead, we hunt for context. Searching for the answer as if we don't know the way. Dungeons and Dragons Ranger class on the mission, but it's not like we're weaving through the forest sniffing plants for the sight of the footprintless one. There. He went that way.

LYLE: How much?
KURT: I really just need a gram, but might as well buy in bulk, get the price break. Quarter?
LYLE: I'm running low too. Might as well get the half.
KURT: Holler.
LYLE: Alright I'll text her now. When you need it by?
KURT: I mean, whenever.

Then I wait ten days. At least once during every single one of those days Tex messages me on Twitter direct message—which is our preferred method of communication as Tex is usually sitting in front of his computer and doesn't receive texts. It's never a nagging presence like where is the stuff or when are we doing this? or please dear god keep me updated I am desperate for a road trip. More of a hello, what's up, how's your life. Normally about something else entirely. On one day he tries to get me to sign his petition for the Criterion Collection to release *Gummo* but I don't do it because I don't believe "fan pressure" is the answer or the Criterion will just be a mouthpiece for nerd culture curtailing their demands to what the people want. The people are stupid. They want Dr. Who on Criterion or some shit. That's not even a movie, it's a TV show. Every time I message him I say something cryptic so as to not talk about buying drugs on an app that I know goes straight to the NSA. Stuff like: no news yet and sorry man still haven't heard from my guy and when I know you'll know. Sometimes Tex gets confused and doesn't understand my fragments and I have to explain further without explaining fully.

Eventually Lyle calls me. He apologizes for the delay, but it turns out they had to put down his nineteen year old dog so he'd been relatively predisposed and just remembered that I'd asked him for drugs. Crispy had had a good life but it was time. So he'd been dealing with that, but repeated apologies anyways (because he's just that kind of guy) for not being able to help deal with the drug dealing. I told him to not to worry about it and take his time, but he assured me that he'd properly mourned, plus drugs would help. Come on over, he said, his girl was on her way. Bring cash. I was kind of sad about not being able to say bye to Crispy. Really was a good boy.

It's happening, I message Tex, but don't wait for a reply. Hop in the car, drive out of the way to an ATM, withdraw $500 dollars, hoping that's enough but knowing that Lyle will cover the difference if it isn't, get lunch, and make my way back to the neighborhood and find a parking spot directly in front of his house all before his girl arrives. One of those doors that is never locked so I make my way inside to see his wife and his roommate lounging and watching a movie on cable. Two dogs bark at me instead of three. Nic Cage says "I'm gonna steal the Declaration of Independence" and walks away. A moment, Justin Bartha laughs, says, "Uh Ben?" and then follows after. Cuts to a car commercial, and I'm able to shake my head loose from the attention-grabbing national treasure that is *National Treasure*. Lyle emerges from the back room.

LYLE: You just missed her.
KURT: I just missed her?
LYLE: In and out. But I fronted you for the K. No worries.

This is why she's not my girl. Elusive. Just as I think today's the day that I get proper facetime and get to introduce myself and say something about needing her number and then she puts it in my phone and I call it when I need drugs instead of calling another guy to call her and waiting ten fucking days because it's not my timetable but his. This will all be recounted to Tex in a car in the future, but now it's just in my head. Save it for the screen, I remind myself.

KURT: How much do I owe you?

Lyle pauses while doing mental math in his head. Watching his lips move, mumbling to himself numbers and divisors when I'm pretty sure it's just whatever he paid divided by 2. $325. I pay him $340. Tip the man for his effort, and not shaft the guy $5 because I can't make change.

LYLE: You wanna do a bump?
KURT: Oh for sure.

We do. From his bag, because he's generous like that. Sharing spoons and zoning out in front of the couch, we finish the movie. Not until the channel suggests we stick around for *National Treasure 2: Book of Secrets* that I admit to having to book it, myself. Thank Lyle for the help and drop one meep of a sorry about Crispy on my way out the door.

- NEVADA -

<u>TEX</u>

I'm depressed. I'm annoying. I get it. I message people too much. I want people to sign my stupid petitions. I beg for people to recognize me, to love me, to respect me, to understand that I am good at what I do. But I don't want to do anything anymore. I'm bored with everything—including this thing I'm writing.

What Kurt isn't saying is that we're disguising this as a book tour. My book that people both like and hate, and his book that hasn't come out yet—or wait… Has it come out? Maybe it has. Fuck. We usually hype each other up—though Kurt has taken to trolling me more lately. More so now that he knows I'm falling into a pretty heavy depression. A book tour for books no one really reads. A cross-country drug run to a person we've only talked to online. But for me, it's an end of the tour tour. I'm either quitting words or quitting everything after it's all over.

Call me dramatic—whatever. I am. This is what I take meds for. I'm depressed. I'm annoying. I'm often a little bitch. People tend to get annoyed with my presence. People go "Yeah, I like him" until they download more of my bullshit into their mental feeds and then search desperately for the MUTE THIS CONVERSATION button.

I've been eating too much cereal lately. My clothes don't fit like they used to.

See, even this is annoying. It's just me bitching, whining, not at all talking about what's going to happen or what's happening. Kurt introduced everything all nice and fun like and here I am, pissing myself off—I can't even imagine how much it's pissing you off. But like there *is* a plot here, I guess. A road trip narrative we're trying to put together. So I guess I'll stop the loathing and get right into the fear. Fuck Everything And Run. Okay.

So I ate Chinese food last night from a place called China Good II and today my farts are bubbly. Like when there's about a half-inch of water in the bathtub and you mash your asshole against the bottom of the tub and rip a chunky assburp. Except there's no tub, no water. Just my ass blasting nasty wet sounds. I'll be like this for the next two or three days. Not the best way to start our book tour/drug run/end of narrative thing.

My partner gives me a mullet before the tour.

We've decided to take my car because it's newer—a 2017 white Nissan Versa with like 45k miles on it—and I've just got an oil change and new tires and brakes and all that. They recommended I get my brake fluid flushed and my timing belt changed, but fuck that. They always tell me to do that. But Kurt lives in San Diego and I live in Las Vegas and so he'll drive here on Wednesday night, late. He'll sleep on my couch and we'll wake up early—*hella fuckin early*—in Kurt's words, and we'll start out East. Most people head West in things like this. West to the Promised Land of California, Los Angeles, Hollywood, the Land Where My Weary Soul Can Connect With Other Weary Souls and We Can Finally Be Free. Big Sur and all that. But we're heading East. To the cold Atlantic. To America's trashy penis—Florida. The Land Where Headlines Read **Naked Man on Bath Salts Saves Dog From Gator's Jaws In Wendy's Drive-Thru, Then Robs Store, Gets Away On PowerWheel.** They have very long headlines in Florida. Adaptation at its finest.

I need to stop sitting at my computer all day.

I won some money recently. Twenty thousand dollars for a screenplay about—meh, who cares what it's about. It's a road trip movie. But so I won money for it. I gave half to my partner. Because they don't really know I probably won't come back. And I want them to be okay. Ten thousand is enough to help them for a little while, right? It has to be, because I'm taking the other ten thousand to do this trip. Ten thousand is hardly enough to go out with a bang, but I think it's enough to have an interesting time along the way. Well, ten thousand minus the $754 it cost me to fix the car.

I ask Kurt if I should go bet a thousand on hard eight, see if I can make some more money. He says *Sure*, but I know he means *It's a stupid idea so don't do it because you have that thousand now and sure you could have like eighteen thousand if you hit hard eight but you could also have nothing if you don't.* He's right. So I've really got $9,246. That's enough. It's gotta be.

I've been having a dream lately where I'm in the middle of nowhere, on the side of the road. Walking. Woods on the right.

Field on the left. And something comes at me really fast. Not a car. A figure. A shadow. Maybe a dog. A human-shaped dog. But like a negative image. A dog burned into the exposure of the reality around me. And then I end. A part of me knows this is how I die—maybe. It's probably just a dream.

On the way, we have both planned and unplanned stops. We've given ourselves time to do the America thing that people did in like the 60s and 70s on motorcycles. Roswell is on the way. I've been there before and it's an embarrassing place, but in a good way. Pretentiously entertaining little Marfa. Austin, Texas—a city that says *Look, we're weird* but actually isn't weird at all. How weird can you be when Jimmy Kimmel hosts his show from there.. My hometown is on the way. I haven't seen my family in years.

So yeah… I'm depressed.

KURT

Las Vegas is five hours away but I drive it in five and a half. One brief stop for fuel—for both me and my whip—I get Arby's and my 2008 silver Scion XB gets Unleaded Regular. Curly fries for the both of us though. I eat while the car takes its own form of sustenance and then we continue on our way.

Driving by the Las Vegas strip is nice because I have fond memories there even if I have approximately zero interest in going back. I first tried ecstasy on a speedway just a couple of miles from here and went to some strip club for my bachelor party where the stripper who gave me the most attention smelled really nice. Still remember that smell if I'm being honest with myself and not my wife.

Tex tells me the plan is to leave in the morning. 13 hours til Roswell so if we're gonna look at some chintzy middle-of-nowhere roadside attraction based around a government cover-up then we'll have to leave by 6AM. Full on pressure, but whatever, if a road trip isn't stressful then what is it? We can't all be-bop back and forth from Denver to New York and then to Denver and to California and back to Denver on the way back to New York.

Consider doubling back and renting a $30 room at the Hooters hotel and waiting til morning to get to Tex's, but he and his partner are waiting for me and I don't want them to think I don't like them. Sure, we're driving thousands of miles together (which is something I'd only be willing to do with a handful of people), but Tex already thinks I don't like him 40% of the time and it feels like this indiscretion (his words, imaginatively at least) would trigger the floodgates of self-doubt and start things off horribly where we'd have to spend hours of driving making amends instead of being friends. Plus the light of the Luxor is far in my rearview and they have already assured me we'd order some good Thai, watch a movie, and call it early. Maybe it'll be a road trip movie, maybe not. Seems obvious.

Stop in their guest parking spot at an apartment complex that sprawls like only complexes do. Take a moment to stare off into nothingness. Alone without any thoughts before my mouth runs non-stop in order to fill the pressure of silence. Grab my backpack, throw it over my shoulder and climb stairs to a door with a number on it that I won't put in print for fear of doxxing my friend and his partner. Phone up and shooting, capturing the start of the documentary—the moment where friends meet like that scene in the first episode of every season of the *Real World*. I ring the doorbell and V answers with a hug and a hello and a come on inside, although not the kind of cinematic opening I'd hoped for. Stop recording and ask them how they've been. We catch up and it's pleasant. Tex emerges, bedraggled.

We don't watch *Road Trip* or *Bubble Boy* or *Fix Daddy* or *Green Book* or *Vacation* or *Little Miss Sunshine* or *Tommy Boy* because we don't need the inspiration. Instead we watch Robert Downey Sr.'s *Greaser's Palace* because it's described as an acid-western and Tex likes westerns and I like acid. We don't make it five minutes before V excuses themself to the bedroom and wishes us luck on our trip tomorrow. Thanks from me and a kiss from Tex and we're hitting play again only to pause it a few minutes later after I ask if Tex wants to do a bit of ketamine. I mean, I know I'm going to, but would Tex like to join?

Tex hems and haws and I'm like come on bro, you've got to try the stuff that this entire narrative arc—er, I mean documentary—is built around and he's like yeah you're right, caving quicker than a mine after it's been blown-up with dynamite, offering that classic line that every anti-drug commercial starts with: but just a little bit though. And I'm like yeah, of course, I'm practiced, baby, ain't trying to k-hole you on the first run triple diamond black ski course and then have you never return to the mountain. Stay in the cabin sipping hot tea saying boy I hate fun while Cavin and I take the slopes. Who even knew they had snow in Florida? Forget to take out a camera to inaugurate this event. Forget about the movie even though we do hit play again. Instead we laugh at ourselves trying to decipher a film that was probably nonsense to begin with. Harder on drugs, but also most definitely sillier. Were the funny things already funny or are they funnier because we've broken down our inhibitors and receptors and are effectively disassociating laughter where there might not have been before? Doesn't matter.

When bedtime comes I make damn sure to put myself into a k-hole once the lights are off and Tex says see you in the morning and I say you too. Well, after I've relieved my bladder and then tried to relieve it once more cause I'm getting to that age. In that moment where I'm nestled in comfy pants and not the same denim that got me here. After hitting play on some foreign film from Tex's subscription of the Criterion channel. Subtitles always lull me right to sleep. Finally. It's a deep spoon, dug in the bag with a mighty heft, but I know how to ride the line between too much and not enough, not daring to show how good I am at this very tightrope act of drug abuse in front of a first-timer. Glad to play host instead of drifting off into the psychedelic realm of WHAT and HAHA and scaring Tex off from wanting to do any more later. The story of the tortoise and the hare goes—

But I lose the analogy and drift off into the clouds, soundtracked by a language I can't understand making me giggle in a way that's decidedly not xenophobic and entirely the circumstances of substances. This couch is far more comfortable than it has any right to be, my body sinking in deeper and deeper until I've become part of it. Lay flat in the fabric, I am immobilized by my choices, but we've got far enough to go tomorrow to worry about that tonight.

CAVIN FUCKING GONZALEZ
(just kidding, it's Bryce, Cavin Bryce Gonzalez)

Ain't shit been the same since I got sober. Ain't shit change either, but that's different shit. Life is not like a box of chocolates. Life is like a series of various Shits—some metaphorical, some literal. Whatever. There's just so much fucking shit. All day. All day I'm looking around like: Look at all this shit. I wake up and my dog farts. Shit in my face. Little microscopic shit literally flying into my fucking face. Clothes all over the floor, just some Shit. I walk outside and see little Shits with faces and names, not that I know them, just existing. In my neighborhood? Audacity!

What I mean is: I hate being sober. It wasn't always like this. I got drunk and acted a fool. My girl left me. She said I was cruel. I was, probably, I don't remember. Shit. So I was like: *Okay. Fuck it. Last year I was drunk and suicidal and I was going to save up money and buy a gun then go somewhere cool and shoot myself* [**DISCLAIMER:** you can get a gun for, like, $300 but I make very little money at work, $300 is a lot of money. And I wasn't going to kill myself with some cheap ass, loser bitch gun. Nah. I wanted a Judge Revolver. Big and hulking, a hand cannon to blast my fucking brain back into space] *and then this year I was going to get married and have kids and find peace. Or I found peace, and love, and instead of killing myself I was going to get married and cum inside of this perfect little angel and make little me's then die the old* *fashioned way: in a lot of pain and probably alone but after having procreated and married. You know what? Fuck this. I am so fucking sick of being some drunk loser that keeps ruining his life.* And then I was sober. And I loved it, at first. When you're high off change. When Shit changes, man. You feel good. Exercise. Eat good. What's this, a full eight hours of sleep? Yeah my cock is huge. That's how being freshly sober feels, like you have a pringles can for a cock and you can't stop showing people your salads. But it withers, man. Quickly. And before long I was depressed, suicidal, AND sober. Yo—what the fuck?

And now here I am. Shit has changed I guess. I don't drink, for starters. I eat more. People seem to like me more, but I don't really like them at all.

And some Shit hasn't changed.

A list of some shit that hasn't changed: my job, my house, my incessant dead end place in human society, the desire to drive my car into a bank and explode on everyone's money out of envy, and my (EX) girl still won't talk to me. She's not even mad, man, she's disappointed. And the worst of the shit that never changes, but I'm addicted to it, that's the internet. Twitter. Fuck. I love to hate Twitter. Fuck you. Kiss me?

Change. Fuck. Shit needs to change. Then it's there, it's just there. Like that angel I fell in love with, singing to me, it's a direct message.

KKUURRTT: Yo—where in Florida are you at?

CAVIN FUCKING GONZALEZ: Orlando, whassup.

KKUURRTT: Me n Tex going on tour.

KKUURRTT: Me n Tex have Ketamine.

Ah, I see, I see. My message was received. See—here's the thing about being sober. I'm not. I'm not sober, like, completely. You know? My problem was with boozing. Drinking. Getting sloshed up and then aggressively tearing down the foundations of my own happiness like it was my fucking job. So, whatever. I can *DO* drugs. I just choose not to drink. You understand this addict psychology?

So I was like, shit. I don't like smoking weed anymore, it stresses me out. And I can't drink. And nobody has good acid. Fuck MDMA. Fuck stimulants—*period*. What I need... What I need is some new perspective. Two brand new, sparkling eyeballs stapled to a brand new, refurbished brain. And then maybe the color wil sleep back in. Maybe I can get back into being really horny over being hydrated and taking vitamins again if I can just synthetically inject a new perspective into my spirit/soul/tongue/veins/whatever. Mushrooms were out. DMT left me scarred for life.

But I wanted drugs, a new drug, one of the three on Earth I hadn't tried yet. So I was like, hey Twitter, SEND ME DRUGS. And I thought it was funny. I was like Haha, now my followers know that being sober is balls haha and I'm fiending haha and the world is crushing me down haha please haha escape haha me? Escape?

And my angels, singing, fuck.

Kurt and Tex. They had Ketamine. Ketamine? What the fuck is that! I don't know.

CAVIN FUCKING GONALEZ: Let's do Ketamine then stop writing forever and retire art and all three of us, we can experience Peace and Love and move to Wisconsin and give all this up. Let's do it. Let's change our lives.

KKUURRTT: Lol

TEX: That's stupid let's just do the Ketamine.

TEX: Hm...

And I could hear that singing, those angels, and my arms began to tingle. My [continue jizzing here]...

- ARIZONA -

<u>TEX</u>

Maybe I'm not that depressed. Because once we get in the car and get on the freeway, a weight lifts and I laugh at almost everything Kurt says. I don't know if it's the ketamine doing it's thing in my brain or if it's the idea that saying goodbye to my partner and kid, giving them both hugs, telling them I love them like it's the last time I ever will, all of it creates this openness to the future and an openness to the end that's absolutely going to come at the end of all this that allows me to let go of that weighted feeling that I'm an annoying depressed piece of shit.

I love seeing a full tank of gas. It says *You can go this many miles in any direction you want without having to stop.* We zipped through the Weinerschnitzel drive through so now the car's full of about two dozen breakfast dogs, three large iced coffees, two chili-cheese fry burritos, and six hashbrowns. We'll snack on all this as the day goes—except the coffee. That's gone before we're out of Nevada.

We pass the Hoover Dam at high speed because yeah it's cool but really who cares cuz it's a dam and not really light enough out for us to take in the view.

> TEX
> Where can I get some damn bait?

KURT

Where can I get some damn dam?

TEX

Damn you.

KURT

What'd I do?

I get intrusive thoughts real bad when I'm on road trips. Also when I'm holding small animals. I try not to think the way a psychopath would but that's got the same logic of the *don't think about eating toenails* thing. But on road trips I always make up scenarios where the person I'm with only wanted to get me on the road so they could take me out to some middle of nowhere place, tie me up, and torture me—bash my head in and eat my brains, cut my dick off and shove it down my throat. I don't think these things are real, but they happen. Especially after Kurt and I watched this short film called *Free Jazz* that talked all about this.

I need to stop thinking like this. I need to take in the sights. We're doing the America thing and here I am thinking about death and torture. This is a good thing. And if at the end of it I'm still thinking about death then that's the time to think about it. Not any time between now and then.

The sun finally crests the horizon, bright and brassy, as we enter the Tucson, AZ city limits. I notice two people standing high on a hill overlooking the freeway—a very tall woman and a man in a wheelchair. I want to point them out to Kurt but he's on his phone, tweeting that we're now in Tucson. How do you get a man in a wheelchair on top of a mountain? I know Tucson is a hub of fitness freaks, so I guess this is a good first sign that that rumor is totally true. Unless they're up there up to no good.

We stop at a Whataburger across from the Randolph Tennis Center and get two more coffees, big ones loaded with cream and sugar. I haven't had Whataburger in like five years so I get a taquito—bacon, egg, and cheese—and an A-1 Thick N Hearty burger for later.

Something's wrong with my brain. I find myself spelling things like *crocodile* as *corciclde* and see nothing wrong with it. My right hand shakes uncontrollably every so often. I can't convince myself that I shouldn't drive on the left side of the road. I can't remember what day it is. I can't remember anything about a book I've just finished.

Kurt shoots footage of Tucson, the mountains, the road. He turns the camera on me and I sing a few lines to a Phil Collins song. He asks:

> KURT
>
> Did you ever think you'd be going on a book tour?

> TEX
>
> Never. Did you know David Foster Wallace used to live in Tucson?

KURT

Is that important to you?

TEX

No. But we're kinda like moving through history, you know? Especially with this whole book thing we're doing. It feels...

KURT

What?

TEX
(doing an impression of
a k-holed David Arquette
from *You Can't Kill
David Arquette*)
Feels so fucking doooope.

Kurt stops filming and takes a sip of his coffee, spilling most of the sip on his shirt. I laugh and sip my own coffee only to do the exact same thing.

KURT

Been mixing up Google Drive and Google Maps a lot lately, and so, when I open Drive instead of Maps I laugh at myself for being too logical for my own good. Yes, you are driving. Smart brain. Smart. Back to Maps, trying to suss out where the fuck Tex is going. It seems like Tucson is a detour that just doesn't add up. Here I'd figured Tex being a Southern boy and all would know the way long enough without winging it. Maybe he does. I'm sure it doesn't matter. We'll get there.

Feel a pang of guilt as we push East past the Tucson city limits. Have friends here that I'm sure would appreciate a hello or a hug. Truth is we've lost touch. Used to see each other three or four times a year, doing drugs while music played on stages. Grown so much from the last time we kicked collective dust around a campground. Now I'm a writer. I mean I was a writer then too, but I've changed characters to build my personality on something beyond "being fun." Hard to live up to. Still down with the drugs though. Obviously. I text David Jack Lim —another three named David in Tucson, hmmm—and say passing through sorry for not stopping. I don't receive a response until a week and a half later when I'm back in California. We catch up. It's nice. Can definitely use the serotonin boost.

I offer to drive, but Tex assures me that he has it he has it.

Can't look at my phone or I'll get car sick, so I just look out the window and observe the different kinds of cacti pass us by. Some of these tall-armed suckers are thousands of years old, and it's only in these long stretches of nothing that I'm able to understand how dinosaurs actually existed. Picture a T-Rex and Brontosaurus roaming the vastness. Oh no, Tyrannosaur is catching up to his prey, jaws clenching around that long neck. Bronto fights back. They're up against the ropes, choke-slamming each other back and forth, a pile driver for good measure, and just sweating it out, desperately waiting for the referee to call tap out on the three count. The ref is obviously a Stegosaurus. He blows the whistle once REX has THE NECK pinned, tearing at it's flesh until the head is completely detached. He swings it around victorious.

I'm so fucking bored. Not a great omen. We talk about people we know and people we don't: filmmakers and friends, internet personalities and other writers. Exclusively shittalk. Better count your blessings if your name didn't come out of our lips. Pass a town called Lordsburg and check Maps again. It says we've got just shy of 5 hours until Alien Paradise. See by millimeter on the map that we're close to Mexico and I suggest a detour.

At the border crossing, we're denied. Two men confounded why these white boys would be trying to cross the border nowhere near any of the good parts of the country. Turns out you need a passport, a thing neither of us knew despite living a mere 20 miles from Tijuana. An hour later, after returning to the route, is when I realize.

KURT: Are we fucking morons?

TEX: What do you mean?
KURT: Uh, DUH?

I pull out the powder and dangle it in front of his face. Tex starts to cackle, wheezing out of breath like I've never seen him react before. He has to pull the car over to the shoulder until he's able to collect himself. He wipes a tear away from his eye.

TEX: Dear God.
KURT: Whoops.

We continue on our way, changing the topic of conversation to people and places that make us happy instead of furious, overjoyed that we're not in an ICE detention center for the rest of our known lives. The little things.

- NEW MEXICO -

TEX

We're somewhere around the turn off to Albuquerque on the edge of the home stretch to Roswell when I shit my pants. I say something like *I feel a little lightheaded; maybe you should drive.* And suddenly there's this terrible *blarp* from my gut and the car fills with a smell we can see, flapping brown inkblots all swooping and screeching up our noses, embedding itself in the fabric of the car—which is going about a hundred miles an hour.

Nah—I just shit my pants. I half-stand, foot on the gas, lifting my ass off the seat. Ease the car into a rest stop that just happens to be right where we need it. Kurt gags, puts his shirt over his nose.

KURT

I'm about to pass out.

TEX

I'm going to get murdered in there.

KURT

Good.

The rest stop looks like any rest stop you'd see in horror movies titled *Rest Stop* and *2 Rest 2 Stop,* and *Rest Stop 3: Rest In*

Pieces and *Rest Stop 4: Dream Warriors*. There's a mud-covered station wagon parked near the women's side of the rest stop that looks less like a station wagon and more like a sentient, extraterrestrial entity assuming the form of an earthy vehicle to lure in unsuspecting victims. We'd probably pay attention to it if it weren't for the shit in my pants.

I don't need to go into detail about what comes next. We all know. But I change into the only other pair of pants I brought for this trip, so it looks like I'm going to be wearing the same pants for three weeks—unless I buy some, which is both a waste of money and also maybe a necessary purchase.

Back on the road we pass by this mountain I recognize. I point to it. Kurt looks at it like it's just another boring mountain that took so long to grow into what it is it can only be measured in geologic time.

                    TEX
See that mountain?

                    KURT
Which one?

                    TEX
The big one.

                    KURT
They're all big.

TEX

When I left Texas on my way to San Diego, I drove all night alone in this packed U-Haul. And it was just before sunrise, the sky this neutral gray-blue color. And I drove past that mountain right there, except I was heading West. And I shit you not, right as I drove past, this meteor broke through the atmosphere, burned a bright golden green, streaked across the sky right above that mountain and then disappeared. I took it as a sign that what I was doing was what I was supposed to be doing. That things would be okay.

We both stare at the mountain as we take the exit for Roswell and ease off I-10, both of us waiting for another meteor to streak across the sky above the mountain and give us a sign that what we're doing is good and that we'll be okay. We exit I-10. Kurt keeps his eye on the mountain in the side-view mirror. I don't think he ever sees a meteor.

What I don't tell him is that I'm thinking of the last meal I had with my parents before I left Texas for good. We went to a Chinese buffet we all used to go to when I was a kid. Dragon in green neon. Lion statues guarding the entrance. And inside I watched both my unhealthy parents eat an unhealthy amount of unhealthy food with their unhealthy son. Intrusive thoughts told me they wouldn't be alive when I saw them again. As much as the meteor felt like a blessing, that last dinner with my parents felt like an omen. Like I was giving up on them. They're still very much alive.

In Roswell, we go to the McDonald's that's shaped like a big

UFO if only to say we went to the McDonald's shaped like a big UFO. We go to a store that's famous for it's owner—a guy who had a son abducted by a UFO thirty years ago. We go in and listen to his tearful, heartfelt story about how, during a night hunt, small, shapeless figures emerged from a bright light and took his son away to a dimension between dimensions. Since then, he's been on the hunt for his son, hiring storyboard artists to draw the scenes, private detectives to search for clues, and stuff like that.

As soon as we leave the shop:

KURT

He totally killed his son, right?

TEX

Totally.

Even though a part of me totally believes that his son was abducted by UFOs because I'm one of those who believes. Probably a by-product of growing up with *Unsolved Mysteries*. Robert Stack. UPDATE.

TEX

You wanna go camp at the crash site?

KURT

Sure.

But my car isn't capable of getting to the crash site. The ruts in the road are too deep. We'll get stuck or rip a hole in my oil pan and put an end to our cross-country drug run book tour road trip.

We still stay the night in the alien city. Kurt wants to stop at a smoke shop called AREA 420 to see if he can score some LSD because how could anyone working at a place called AREA 420 not know where to score some LSD.

It's a dingy place. U-shaped. Glass cabinets. A bead-covered doorway leading to the back. A twelve foot albino python curled in the corner under an army of red-tinted heat lamps. After about five minutes, Kurt gets what he wants and I manage to put six copies of my book on the counter. They give me $5 a copy and price them at $15.

We check into the Roswell Inn—a room with two double beds. They both have the insert-a-quarter massaging bed thing. We jokingly lay in our separate beds, insert quarters and laugh for the first minute or two as the bed vibrates violently. Then we both pass out.

We never lock the door.

KURT

Awoken by a bright light. When I first looked at the clock it was 3:15 and now it's 4:45. Where did time go? What happened? Why does my brain hurt? I remember—zap. Nah, I'm just playing. Tex stands in the bathroom taking a piss. He apologizes for the volume of his stream but I just tell him to turn off the fucking light.

TEX: Sorry. Sorry.

We hit every gift shop in town before finally circling back to the first one, simply titled: Alien Zone. I buy four t-shirts, a commemorative alien etched beer glass, a diorama of a UFO abducting a cow, a patch that reads OFFICIAL UFO HUNTER, a blu-ray box set of the Alien Quadrilogy, an ALF puppet, an alien fetus preserved in a jar, a green baseball hat with two teardrop-shaped alien eyes on the crown, a framed photograph of a UFO signed by Jacques Vallée, fifteen postcards, another t-shirt, a pair of sweatpants with a string of alien faces running down the leg, bigfoot socks, some neon green christmas lights, and a keychain.

I flirt with the girl behind the counter. She's cute and gives me a 10% discount. Her way of flirting back, I guess. Hollers to her manager that she's gonna take her fifteen now and ten of those next fifteen minutes are spent with me, making out next to a dumpster until I get a text from Tex asking where the hell I am. I stammer. It's okay, go, she says, lighting up a cigarette and letting it rest seductively on the edge of her lip. Maybe come see me on your way back through, she says.

Grab my bags and meet back up with Tex who's pumping alien unleaded into his car. He asks where I've been and I don't have much of an answer. Don't particularly feel like telling him that I just cheated on my wife, so we just hit the road and leave it unsaid. Sun's setting by the time we kick off.

- TEXAS -

<u>MARFA</u>

What kind of road trip is it without visiting Marfa? Marfa thinks to itself as KURT and TEX drive right past its exit without even considering stopping.

Marfa depressed.

CAVIN FUCKING GONZALEZ

You know, I tried the regular medication route. To find that beautiful new perspective, I mean. To find the colors I was longing for in an Rx. I tried this route twice. The first time was really, really bad. Like really bad. Just, fucked. The guy was so stupid. His name was Sean. Just kidding. It was Shawn. Shawn, reader. With a fucking W.

Shawn. Fucking Shawnnnnnnnnnnnnn ughhhh. Shawn is like my age but he smells better and by better I mean like an actual baby. He smells like a baby, it's fucking bizarre. Very unsettling. And his glasses. And his cardigans. Ughhhhhhhhh. Shawn. Fucking Shawnnnnnnnnnnnnn ughhhh.

Shawn is my psychiatrist/psychologist. He thinks I have what is called: "Suicidal OCD." It's all very redundant. Our last conversation went like this:

INT. THERAPIST'S OFFICE - DAY

                    SHAWN
          We could try exposure therapy. It's like, let's say
          you wanted to get used to being in ice water.
          Everyday you dip your toes into colder and colder
          water. And then up to your ankles, shins, knees.
          You understand?

CAVIN

You want me to think about killing myself so I don't kill myself?

SHAWN

Haha, you're so funny Cavin Fucking Gonzalez. I wish I were as funny and handsome as you. But yes, I mean that is put rather crudely, but yes I would like you to think about killing yourself in order to avoid killing yourself. It's all very sophisticated, see—

CAVIN

Shawn, I'm thinking about killing myself right now. See that window?

CAVIN POINTS TO A LARGE GLASS WINDOW DECORATED WITH A PRECARIOUSLY PLACED BULLSEYE IN THE CENTER

SHAWN, ALARMED, SITS UP IN HIS CHAIR.

CAVIN

[AFTER JUMPING UP QUICKLY AND PRETENDING TO RUN TOWARD THE WINDOW ONLY TO INSTEAD STAND BESIDE IT, STARING OUT OF IT, BASKING IN THE GLOW LIKE A LAZY FUCKING CAT OR A LOVER AWAITING THEIR PARTNER'S RETURN FROM WAR]

CAVIN (CONT'D)

Hahaha, nah just kidding. But I'm not. Shawn, Shawn. Ughhhh, haha, Shawn. I think about killing myself all the time. That sounds dumb, really. Exposure therapy? I literally am existing all the time as an exposure to illness. Suicidal thoughts are like air. I breathe em in *deep breath*, marvel at em for a second, breathe out *deep breath out*.

SHAWN
[VISIBLY UNCOMFORTABLE]
I don't think you're giving me a chance, here, really. Have a seat and let me explain—

CAVIN

Shawn, remember that medication you recommended I go on?

SHAWN

Yes! Have you looked into it? I really, seriously, really, think it could help.

CAVIN
[CONSULTING DR. GOOGLE VIA PHONE]
It says the side effects can include suicidal urges, ideation, depression. Shawn, what the fuck.

CAVIN
[WHILE STARING AT A WATERFALL, TO HIMSELF]
What the fuck am I doing here?

SHAWN
[WHILE MOVING CAVIN AWAY FROM
THE WINDOW AND TOWARDS THE
TRANQUIL WATERFALL]
You're getting help, Cavin. From me. Believe it or
not, I am a specialist. I have helped so many
people just. Like. You. And I could help you, too.

**[how can we go about making this an obvious daydream
with screenplay typesetting? i imagine something has to
exist to dictate, like, "this is not really happening" —
KKUURRTT]**

**[uhhh… what if we put the next section all in italics or
something? —Tex]**

[try it —KKUURRTT]

*Upon being compared to other people Cavin snaps, stands, and begins
beating the shit out of Shawn. Fuck you fuck you fuck you. Fucking
exposure therapy. Fucking stupid, suicide medication. I'm not overly
compulsive, I don't organize shit! Cavin begins destroying the office,
smashing the vase and table with the hatchet he had been hiding inside his
now seemingly very suspicious trench coat. THERAPY IS FUCKING
STUPID AS FUCK!!!! WHY DO I PAY YOU PEOPLE
WHAT THE FUCK!! Cavin sees the waterfall, he inches closer and
raises his hatchet. Shawn cries like a little baby, No! Please fucking please
not my waterfall please, no, God, anything, anything but the waterfall!
Cavin unplugs the waterfall. The water stops flowing. Cavin's face is calm,
stoic. He stands on the leather armchair he had just been resting on and
begins pissing all over the room, even on Shawn who is crying like a little*

baby. Oh you going to cry you little baby bitch? You smell like a fucking baby Shawn, now cry like one! And be covered in piss like one! Cavin finishes pissing and texts the groupchat he's in: Going to Jail lol or Prison? Idk one. He gets a reply: Lol, therapy? Cavin looks about the now flaming room and the weeping, piss soaked Shawn, "I'd rather die... than go to Jail," he says, and then picks up the waterfall and smashes it so that the shards of decor will exist as the last poem he ever wrote. And then... well, you know the rest. He slits his throat with the hatchet, slits both wrists with the hatchet, then jumps out of the fucking window.

CAVIN
Yeah, Shawn. You're right. I don't know why I'm being so confrontational. I'm sorry. Hey, our times up. But, look. I'm sorry? Okay, yeah. I'm sorry.

SHAWN
Thank you.

CAVIN
And you don't smell like a baby.

SHAWN
I'm sorry?

CAVIN
No, don't be. Next week... we can start the exposure therapy okay?

Cavin and Shawn passionately make out and then Cavin feels better and gets a better job and a cool new girlfriend and a new house and car and his dog is cooler too somehow and everything is better now because Shawn, Shawn saved him with exposure therapy and a prescription for drugs that *should have by all statistical measurements killed him. Haha, no, just kidding, that didn't happen, he just left. Cavin left and he didn't feel better, at all, although fucking around with Shawn was kind of fun and that almost made him feel better for a bit. Not paying $150 a visit fun, but here we are. And that was the last time he ever heard from Shawn. A week later he got a bill for $900. Apparently Shawn had gotten certified as a specialty specialist of specialties or something and so was worth more money and his insurance didn't cover the specialty services performed by specialists. Fucking therapy man.*

[yeah, i think that worked. —KKUURRTT]

TEX

A road trip is boring and a road trip narrative is even more so —especially when we forget to film most stuff and end up forgetting to stop and do the fun stuff. But it's not long after we get in the car when the silence sets in. And we're both fine with riding the highways silently, don't have to fill every moment with bullshit chatter. Cuz we're legit buds. Sometimes, though, the silence is like *really* boring. We've tried music but our tastes are too different. Like ketchup and ice cream, tuna fish and strawberry milk… and some kind of third combination that's way out there and completes the rule of threes.

I try heavy metal (Lamb of God, Power Trip, Kataplexis, Tony Danza Tapdance Extravaganza, Behemoth, Gojira, Andrew WK, and Meshuggah).

KURT
Fuck no. This shit's gonna give me a heart attack.

So then I try some cheesy shit (Phil Collins, Genesis, Michael Bolton, Go West, Billy Ocean, Chesney Hawkes, Toto, and some Katy Perry).

KURT
You serious with this?

So we beat on, boats against the current, borne ever endlessly into the future, toward an ending—in silence.

KURT

Book tour is going well. Ha. We've sold approximately zero copies but maybe that was by design. Been virtual up to this point anyways, recording videos of us saying "buy my book" in interesting places. Wasted half a day in Roswell, you'd think that's all the footage we have. My book isn't even out yet so it's always just some variation of "pre-order my book" or "buy my book one day" or "maybe I don't even have a book and I'm just lying to you. That seems characteristically in form." Becoming less and less of a documentary and more and more of two millennials grasping onto influencer culture like the last bastion of a thing that can save us from getting old. Mr.'s our father's names.

Hold up the camera anyways and speak into them in voices that would shame ourselves if we weren't already doing them. Saving the footage for later so we can totally edit this into something sensical and not at all what it feels like. Doing readings on the side of the highway shouting over traffic because we forgot the microphones a couple of states back and you can't make a film without proper sound design. Just ask all those guys (and five women) who won the oscar for it when they don't even have one for best stunt performance. The first film to win The Academy Award for sound recording is *It's a Mad Mad Mad Mad World* which we bear few similarities beyond cars moving on roads captured on film. Lots of B-Roll.

Common ground got left approximately a thousand miles back and we shortly realize that we don't have enough shared history to reminisce past a single pass through. Maybe we're great at creating new experiences, we think, stopping at Dinosaur Land where we're both hysterically laughing at the dumb fucking dinosaurs with eyes that don't fit their face. Bad art at it's finest and yet we're back on the road and the silence sets in again. Tried music but we're just too different. Tex wants heavy and I want mellow and neither of us can really stomach the other's taste. Stuck in the middle with nowhere to go and neither of us feeling much like getting rejected again. We're repeating ourselves and change the topic:

KURT: Should we listen to a podcast?
TEX: I don't really do podcasts. We could listen to ours?
KURT: Our podcast? No. I'm not listening to our podcast.
TEX: That's the only podcast I listen to.
KURT: Have you given any others a shot?
TEX: Not really. Just the ones you sent me before we started recording ours. Didn't really do it for me. Just people talking at each other. Don't see the point.
KURT: What about like a nonfiction one?
TEX: Like what?

We scroll and end up on some true crime one about this Texas serial killer named the TEXAS BRO STRANGLER who only targets pairs of men driving across the state west to east like. By the end of the first episode we're sweating. The binge sets in and we're gripping the dashboard like our life depends on it, in the sheer anticipation of the end of it all. Some man with a meathook mutilating us just for the sport of it. For the good old-fashioned chuckle. By episode three we're bored. Or at least I am. Think Tex is just in that perpetual zone in the passenger seat, staring out the window not even really listening in the first place. I wonder if he's been on this stretch of highway before or it's too high or too east, but I don't see much point in asking. I ask instead if he minds if I put on some music and he says whatever, a million miles or just a couple of hundred away. Pause podcast.

Fiddle with my phone, but there's no service out in the middle-of-nowhere fucking West Texas and my only options are what I've already got downloaded—which limits our listening to the entirety of the Grateful Dead's 1972 Europe tour and a playlist labelled "Trip Hop · Chillout · Groove · Downtempo"— neither sound much like the kind of thing that's going to get me through hours of highway sameness. The thing about a road trip is that they sound appealing until it gets to the driving part. Driving driving driving driving driving driving driving driving driving driving some more. I could eat or I could piss or I could drive this car right through that cattle fence and see if Tex's car is an all terrain vehicle or what. Put the podcast back on and listen to three more murders that sounded an awful lot like the three before that. Mental reminder to download some music next time we come across wifi. A precious commodity that seems less significant in the era of 5G LTE.

TEX: See podcasts kinda suck.
KURT: Yeah, but I like the ones that are mostly just bullshiting anyways.
TEX: So let's record one.
KURT: Bullshit?

TEX: Yeah.
KURT: Should we use your phone, or—
TEX: Mine's full.
KURT: Okay

Tex doesn't lift a finger and because of his careless inaction I'm breaking the law in most states. Sorry officer it's not texting and driving, it's tweeting and driving. That's different. Send that tweet off real quick before pulling up the RED voice recording app. I have a BLUE one too, but tend to gravitate toward the RED one. Tell myself it's because we're in a red state but that's not remotely true. Hit record and ask Tex if he's ready even though I've already hit record so it's not like he has much of an option. He says yeah anyways and my voice changes octaves from bored driver to radio douche.

KURT: This is the pilot episode of On Thee Road, a road trip podcast hosted by me, Kurt Kerouac, with as always my partner in pod, Tex Cassady.
TEX: Yup that's me, Tex Cassady. On the Road with the On The Road Podcast.
KURT: The only On The Road podcast recorded while on the road. Currently driving through Texas on our way to Florida. From Heck, Texas to Gosh, Florida.
TEX: Though I think you'd make a better Neal Cassady. I'll be Kerouac...
KURT: Yeah, whatever. I was literally just alliterating. I'll toss that hammer. I don't care.
TEX: So how do you feel about On the Road?
KURT: The book?
TEX: Yeah.
KURT: It's alright. Big Sur is better.

TEX: I like Dharma Bums.
KURT: Haven't read it.
TEX: Well okay then—

We stop and let the silence settle back in like it's the not the thing we're most afraid of and if we write and write and write and write until our hand cramp and our teeth fall out and we become the 84 year-old narcissistic vampire sociopaths that we vowed we'd never become it'll just go away forever. Sure, the silence lingers, and we let it. Dragging out this bit of "having nothing to say" to the point that we forget we were ever even recording. I don't even hit stop and the recording goes—all said and done—hours to go until my battery dies and we settle into a side of the road motel that doesn't not look like the one from *Psycho*. Bluebird has eight rooms and after putting down my credit card for $89.99 plus incidentals, we receive the key for room number four.

Once inside, we set down the bags and Tex asks if I think the guy who works here is the Texas Bro Strangler. I tell him, yeah, probably, but don't pay it any more attention until we're woken in the middle of the night by two bros screaming at the top of their lungs. At least it's not us, I say to myself as I roll over and fall back asleep.

In the morning I wake up first, and while Tex tosses and turns, I upload the six hour file of ON THEE ROAD to the internet. Blast it out to twitter with the text: LISTEN, even though I don't actually expect anyone to.

ANDYWARHOL.COM

The Factory moved out of New York City around the time I got shot. There is a rumor going around that I've got a version of the Factory in over a dozen cities, albeit only ones deemed "second" or "third" tier by those who make those kinds of claims. Your Oklahoma Cities and your Iowa Cities, but not pluralization to represent the multitude of cities in those states, but the pluralization as one would utilize in referring to cities of the type. Truth is, the Factory moved to the cloud. Always was a fan of the internet even before John Perry Barlow talked my ear off about it at a party in '92. He was so droll. I loved him.

I won't dare publish the URL here, because what we've got going is something too special for shameless self promotion. A slew of like-minded souls creating content for the mere thrill of it and not the public adoration. I refer specifically to those under my curation as uninfluencers—those who despite their best efforts seem unable to influence anyone. I like to think of my own art this way, but others found a way to capitalize on what didn't need to be capitalized upon. The money was nice, but the fame wasn't something I felt equipped for. I don't see why I couldn't have lived the party lifestyle without ever actually being seen at the party. I adore wallpaper.

Things pass me by all the time: mixed media from any and all angles every hour of the day. If you could see that number ticking up on my email box by the second you wouldn't bother. I don't want to be adored. I want to be ignored. It's as simple as that. Sometimes you stumble upon something so special though. A screengrab of an Instagram posted to Twitter and then shared to Reddit. An upcycled scene from a film captured in brief motion used to express emotions where words don't have to. A YouTube video with a single view. But nothing of late has made me gasp with shock and glee like this ON THEE ROAD podcast. The exact kind of energy I was going for when I made *Empire* in 1964. Beautiful anxiety captured in silences in slight sounds, the roar of the road and nothing else. This is true art. The rest is just a facsimile.

Don't ask for permission, couldn't be bothered. Instead I re-purpose re-mix re-release these glorious six hours (with credit where credit's due) on the Factory's podcast network: gcpn ("generic corporate podcast network"). Wait for weeks for a second episode, but it never comes, settling instead for this one episode on repeat four times a day, "ad nauseum" as my assistants say. I consider it my muse and start painting again. Start with soup cans because it's comfortable, but Amy's Thai Curry Sweet Potato Lentil doesn't have the same pop as Campbell's Tomato. Did I invent the meme? Are we not all just carbon copies of each other over and over again building personalities as brands and hoping that nobody catches wise that we're secretly frauds. Start writing poetry because it's the only true art form, but I can't give up the limelight and I quickly start reciting those poems on TikTok in front of a self-facing camera. Haters say it's an impersonator.

WORLD'S SMALLEST CATHOLIC CHURCH

I have been taking pictures of the church for the last forty nine years. I moved to Blacksmith, Texas in 1969. One day, driving along the beautiful winding backroads, I discovered the church. No larger than eleven feet by eleven feet. I found myself returning to it every weekend, standing outside the fence to look at it, to imagine all those who have worshipped inside it since its construction in 1888. Three years of visiting and a vision told me to start taking pictures. So I bought a used Nikon in 1972 and started developing my photography skills on the church. In 1984, a friend of mine named Gavin Buckley suggested that I start selling my photos of the barn at the Chapel Hill Bluebonnet Festival and at the monthly artist market in Round Top. Never thought it would bring me any money, but I've made my living off these photos and nothing else. People come from not just distant places in Texas, but also from other states to purchase my photos. With the advent of internet shops, I've even sold prints to different countries—Romania, France, Iraq. My biggest achievement was a profile in the New Yorker about the church which included six of my photos, each purchased for an amount that allowed me to buy my current house.

I'm here at the church today, taking pictures against the sun. I've become fascinated with silhouettes. And this small wonder gives off a silhouette that, combined with the surrounding hill country, the trees and birds, creates this little heaven my lens captures.

Most days, the church and I are alone. I'm allowed to be free with its beauty. I've almost never entered the church in all these years. Maybe today is different. Something about the light hitting the side windows. I think the inside might give me something to capture, finally. It could be a moment—

A car slides to a stop in the gravel outside the church. Kicks up dust. Stops so hard that it almost skids sideways. I jump back, afraid that their car is going to go out of control and either hit me or fly into the church.

Pretty sure I scream.

Two young guys get out. Dirty-looking. Definitely not from Blacksmith, or any of the towns around here. They've got the look of the kind that live in Austin. Not that there's anything wrong with that. I'm as liberal as they come.

I don't say anything. The tall one waves to me with a smile and I put the camera in front of my face like I didn't see him. I snap a picture of them in front of the church and eavesdrop on their conversation because it sounds important. They're going:

"You think anyone sees this church?"

"Once you see the sign for the church, it's no longer about the church."

"Impossible to see it."

I want to say *But it's right there* but a part of me I've never felt tells me this is about so much more than what they're saying.

"We're not here to capture an image, we're maintaining one. Every picture of this church reinforces that aura. It's an accumulation of nameless energies, ya know?"

"We see only what others see, what others take pictures of. The church doesn't really exist. We've surrendered to it. Given it a spiritual devotion. Kinda like all tourism. Everything like this is an image of an image. Never the image of itself because it's what we expect the image to be. What we expect the church to be."

"The World's Smallest Catholic Church. And we'll never see it as anything else."

The tall one looks at me again, then back at the church.

"Like that guy over there, taking pictures of the church. He's taking pictures of taking pictures."

"What do you think the church was like before it was photographed?"

They pause. A silence between them that weighs so heavy on me that I feel tears welling up in my eyes. A tightness in my chest. I want to collapse. To scream and cry. But I can only stand, camera in hand, waiting for what they're going to say next. The shorter one speaks first.

"I can't believe we just sat here, looking at this kinda cool little church, and reenacted a scene from *White Noise* by Donald Delldillo."

"We're so cool."

They get back in their car and peel out, pull a sharp one-eighty and head back in the direction they came. I'll never see them again, never even know who they are. But they have awakened something in me, a primitive sadness that has never been there before. I feel defeated, forgotten. I feel like a lie, like everything I've ever done isn't something I was supposed to do but rather something that was written about without my consent and forced upon me. That the first moment I saw the church, the first picture I took of it, sealed me into a prison of inherently false behavior. I'm a lie. I'm fake. I am not real. Never was. Never will be. I can't even look at the church. The camera weighs heavy in my hand, burning my skin. I throw it into the road. My body aches. Sweat bubbles out of me. A sour stink oozes from my pours, a stink that whispers *Run away*. And so I start walking away from the church, down the road, in a direction where I know nothing is.

TEX

I guess you could say we're kinda sorta writing our version of *The Excellent Mr. Dundee*—that mockumentary about Paul Hogan trying to reinvent himself as an actor other than the guy who played Corciclde Dundee. Except our version isn't really about us reinventing ourselves but rather us reinventing our world into something magical out of the mundane.

I've got like forty-eight places to show Kurt in Austin because I used to live here and I love this place. Gordough's, Pinballz, ~~Vulcan Video~~, ~~I Luv Video~~, the Church of Scientology, Mount Bonnell, Waterloo, ~~Hut's Hamburgers~~, ~~Death Metal Pizza~~, Ramen Tatsu-Ya, The White Horse, Texas Chili Parlor, ~~Magnolia Cafe~~, The Continental Club, Stubs, Mohawk, Book People, ~~Alamo Drafthouse Ritz~~, and on and on. Mostly the hotspots because in Austin even the touristy hotspots are fucking badass. Dig deeper and it only gets better—or that's how it used to be. We've got to at least find Leslie, if they're still alive.

But being fucking writer nerds, we end up at Half Price Books on North Lamar. There's a line outside the shop that we ignore and as we try to push our way inside there's a collective *Hey motherfuckers* and *Get back in line* and *No cutting* and we're like *Shut the fuck up, we're going in here to shop* but no one believes us.

TEX

It's like a corporate-ish used book store that has everything. Pynchon, DeLillo, Burroughs, Dick—

KURT

...David Foster Wallace.

TEX

It's mandatory that every Half Price Books has at least six copies of *Infinite Jest* in stock for all the—

KURT

No... Look.

Kurt points and I follow it to where the line of people begins and see David Foster Wallace, sitting at a small table signing copies of his new book. I haven't read it yet, but heard it's an autofic novel about a depressed writer living in the aftermath of the suicide of his friend/fiercest writing competition— which is clearly about the suicide of Jonathan Franzen.

But there he is, signing books. Gray hair flowing from a pink bandana. Clear acetate glasses slipping halfway down his nose. Vague idea of a beard covering his acne-scarred face. He smiles and hands a signed book to a woman dancing with delight so wildly it looks like she's about to piss her pants.

A sign next to the table reads: **AWP Off-Site Event—David Foster Wallace Reading From His New Book** *You've Changed, Man.* **Book Signing After Reading. Must Purchase Copy of Book from Half Price Books Associate.**

Mr. Wallace Will Not Personalize Autograph. No Photography.

Kurt's got his phone out, filming DFW sign and smile.

                          VOICE
              Tex? Kurt?

I'm always uneasy when anyone calls my name in public. But having Kurt's name attached to mine lets me know it's someone I might want to talk to versus someone I totally don't.

And then I realize it's coming from the intercom.

                    INTERCOM VOICE
              Tex? Kurt? Your coffees are ready at the coffee
              counter.

But before we go collect the coffees neither of us remember ordering, we see Brian Alan Ellis standing in line. Kurt approaches him first.

                          KURT
              Hey BAE, what'd'ya say?

                    BRIAN ALAN ELLIS
              Uh...

                          KURT
              It's Kurt... And Tex... From the internet...

BRIAN ALAN ELLIS
(vague recollection)
Oh yeah... So you cuties here for AWP?

KURT
We honestly didn't know that was going on until just now. Oh shit... We got something for you.

Kurt hurries out the door and I stand there awkwardly with Brian Alan Ellis. I look at the copy of *You've Changed, Man* in his hands.

BRIAN ALAN ELLIS
(clearly embarrassed that he's standing in line to get David Foster Wallace's autograph)
I'm gonna sell it. Pay rent. Get some Applebee's, ya know?

The person behind us gasps as if Brian Alan Ellis has just confessed to being in line in order to assassinate David Foster Wallace. Kurt returns with the ALF puppet and hands it to Brian Alan Ellis.

KURT
We got it in Roswell.

BRIAN ALAN ELLIS
Oh... Uh... Thanks?

He juggles the ALF puppet and the book in his hands. Clearly annoyed. And then, as if things aren't weird enough, Bret

Easton Ellis walks in, storms up to David Foster Wallace's little table. Everyone watches this happen in reverent awe. I assume the confrontation has something to do with a longstanding feud between David Foster Wallace and Bret Easton Ellis regarding their "immeasurable talent" that neither is willing to concede to.

> BRET EASTON ELLIS
> The next time you talk shit about me on Charlie Rose, I'm going to make sure to find everything I can on you and dox the fuck out of you. Do you understand me, forehead?

> DAVID FOSTER WALLACE
> No comprende.

> BRET EASTON ELLIS
> Fuck you, Wallace.

Bret Easton Ellis storms past us and that's when I notice Jonathan Safran Foer gently slide a copy of Pynchon's *V.* back on the shelf and turn away from the crowd—probably grateful no one knows who the hell he is. And wait... Is that Troy James Weaver buying a DVD copy of *Out of the Blue*? What the hell's he doing here? He wouldn't come to AWP. Oh, he's with Nathaniel Kennon Perkins... Makes sense. And then Brian Alan Carr walks away from the David Foster Wallace table with his freshly signed book and he and Brian Alan Ellis give each other the stink eye. And then Fiona Alison Duncan and Rachel Eve Moulton are clearly trying to shoplift rare copies of Harmony Korine's Gagosian catalog. And I notice Fernando A. Flores standing near the front, taking pictures of the whole scene on an analogue camera like he always does—but his presence isn't that weird. He lives here.

> BRIAN ALAN ELLIS
> What the fuck is going on?

> TEX
> It's never like this in here.

> BRIAN ALAN ELLIS
> Like what?

> TEX
> No, I was talking to Kurt.

> KURT
> What'd you say?

> BRIAN ALAN ELLIS
> He said it's not usually like this in here.

> KURT
> What isn't?

> BRIAN ALAN ELLIS
> Can y'all, like, fuck off?

But before we can—

> DAVID FOSTER WALLACE'S HANDLER,
> JENNIFER ELIZABETH JORGENSON
> Next!

And Brian Alan Ellis walks up to David Foster Wallace. Kurt and I follow and the crowd behind us screams and boos and whines *No cutting!* like a bunch of children. And it's in this moment that I'm realizing everyone in line is someone I recognize, here for AWP: Richard Cheim, Lindsay Hunter, John Englhardt, D.T. Robbins, Eugene Lim, Steven Dunn, Nicolette Polek, Colin Winnette, and like twenty other writer —all of them booing at Kurt and I. A dream I've had once, now a reality. I make the cringe emoji face at them.[2]

TEX
Shut up! We don't even have a book for him to sign.

KURT
We're here for moral support.

I see some people who were published by the same press that published my first book. I wave to them. They act like they don't know me. We turn back right as Brian Alan Ellis finishes getting David Foster Wallace's autograph. He walks past us without saying goodbye. David Foster Wallace looks at us, searching for our purchased copies of *You've Changed, Man*— even though we don't have any.

DAVID FOSTER WALLACE
The fuck, guys?

I rip a meaty fart. Kurt looks at me with a smile he reserves for

---

[2] This one —> 😫

the *I can't believe you've done this* moments. And we both look back at David Foster Wallace. A smile quietly smears across his face.

                    DAVID FOSTER WALLACE
            Nice out.

                           TEX
        Amen.

And then his handler shoos us away. Out of earshot—

                           KURT
            I wanna see if he wants to do some drugs with us.

                           TEX
        Nah, man. Let's just get our coffees and go.

                           KURT
        Sure.

And then we spend five minutes looking for the coffee counter before realizing this book store doesn't have a coffee shop in it. What the fuck?

And it turns out ~~Leslie~~[3] died a long time ago. Which depresses me.

---

[3] https://en.wikipedia.org/wiki/Leslie_Cochran — and I'm pretty sure he was McConaughey's inspiration for Moondog in *The Beach Bum*

BRIAN ALAN ELLIS

"Ah, mecca," I announce to nobody as I stroll into the Applebee's Neighborhood Grill + Bar.

I'm getting weird looks from everyone, like I don't belong.

Just kidding.

Nobody cares.

And yes, I fucking do belong.

Nestled inside the ALF hand puppet I'm wearing is my freshly signed copy of the latest David Foster Wallace tome—*You've Changed, Bro*—which, once I sell on eBay, should cover at least two years' worth of rent in the dilapidated punk house my scabby, drug-addicted cat and I currently live at.

I make a mental note to not get any ranch dressing on my new treasure, which would surely bring its value down—the treasure being the DFW book, not the ALF hand puppet that Tex and Kurt so obnoxiously gifted me at the AWP conference.

They were trying to be cute, I'm sure.

Tsk, tsk.

Don't those fools realize that I'm completely over ALF?

I've moved on.

I'm highbrow now.

I collect E.T.

Which they'll get to read about whenever my latest story, "The E.T. Period" drops in the next issue of *The Paris Review*.

Unless of course those brutish simpletons are still just reading online "indie-lit" which they probably are, and shame to them, yuck!

I think they mentioned something about being on a road trip, to film an *Easy Rider* sequel or some such nonsense. (Or was it *End of the Tour 2: Consider the Electric Boogaloo*??)

Tex said they'd gone to Nevada.

I wonder if they hooked up with Noah Cicero, to maybe do peyote in the desert and talk about panda bears and Tao Lin and Buddha or some shit.

Who knows?

Nervously adjusting my turtleneck sweater, I notice how this Applebee's, my safe space, has been overtaken by crummy writers.

I see Don DeLillo putting a pretty massive hurt on a classic combo platter.

There's Lorrie Moore, sloppy off of some 2-for-1 margarita pitchers.

George Saunders has marinara dripping from his stupid professor beard.

And my meal ticket, David Foster Wallace, is playing touch-screen trivia in a corner booth.

These people have ruined literature, and now they're ruining my Applebee's experience.

It's all too much.

Then I look over and see Tex and Kurt entering the fray.

Yikes.

This is my cue to leave.

"Y'all blew it!" I announce while taking the Applebee's hostess (who is goth) by the hand and exiting.

And once the both of us are at a safe distance, the Applebee's explodes into flames as the theme song to *Dog the Bounty Hunter* plays in the background.

Bye, losers!

KURT

Neither of us remember to promote much in the way of our books. Have this one idea where we hold a public reading on Sixth Street with a soap box and a megaphone, but every store we go to is fresh out of megaphones and the soap box store went out of business years ago. We do end up buying one of those dorm-room-sized erasable white boards and writing HECK, TEXAS by TEXT GRESHMAN ($15) and THE UNTITLED KKUURRTT AUTOFIC NOVEL by KKUURRTT (TBA) on it in hopes that someone pays us attention. We forget to film it and end up quickly erasing the sales pitch for jokes that take the precedent of our attention. After a couple of iterations we settle on KEEP AUSTIN WIERD like we can't spell even though we're authors. For some reason this is hilarious to us. Unable to determine whether it's subtlety or just plain old unfunniness that prevents others around us for joining in on the chuckles and chuffaws. But maybe that's just our style.

Hoodwink a couple of poets out of their AWP badges and end up on the conference floor, separating for an hour to go shopping and purchase ourselves a reading slate for the next calendar year. At the booth for **@rlysrslit** I run into [REDACTED] and ask if he wants to do some LSD with me. Tex thinks that I wanted just ANY LSD, which couldn't be further from the truth. In reality I was just extensively curious to see what the people in Roswell got high on. How the alien fanatics went about hallucinating. Fuck a comet, I'm trying to see a UFO. I don't tell [REDACTED] any of this as I split a tab in half between him and myself ripping a tab off the strip, and that tab in half. Have to use my teeth, and while he grimaces, he doesn't seem to lose interest. Quickly lose each other in the hubbub of people buying and selling books. Later I meet up with Tex and tell him what happened. He says that he wants some, but this stuff is pretty heavy and I tell him that I don't recommend. We ARE the aliens.

Can't sleep. High as hell. Watching fractals play out on the roof of yet another hotel room until dawn breaks and it's hopeless to even try turning longform winks into actual, legitimate sleep. Bright lights and flying objects. In the morning, I remain absolutely frying but don't admit it to my travelling companion, hoping that a shower and a solid breakfast will turn the day around. In what only feels like twenty minutes we're in Houston and I'm smiling in my brain but trying not to on my face, head clouded with thoughts that tell me I'm right in the thick of it still.

Stop at Chris's (Tex's childhood friend) house first, before we take a detour over to casa de Gresham. Turns out Tex isn't ready to see his parents quite yet and has to decompress with old friends before committing to a childhood case study. I get it. Right there with you buddy, I say to myself, staring at my palms and not opening the door to follow after him.

TEX: You okay buddy?
KURT: Oh yeah, fine, chilling. You okay?
TEX: I guess. I hate it here.

KURT: Well just do what I do and imagine you don't.

TEX: What?

KURT: I mean maybe once upon a time I was this ball of unerring positivity but I definitely lost my way somewhere over the years. The ability to smile when things sucked. Keep people's names out of my mouth. Live bliss. But I learned how to evolve when people continued to expect it of me. It's not faking it. It's imagination.

Tex looks me over like he knows I'm high. I think that made sense. Fuck, I was just trying to help. Shouldn't have said anything at all. But he takes a deep breath, closes his eyes for approximately 3.3 seconds and says okay I think I can do this thanks.

Inside, we sit in Chris's basement and it's an exact replica of my cousin Johnny's. I don't know which cousin black belt Johnny actually is: first, second, third so I just round up to the general idea of cousin. Pool table, three pinball machines (*Creature From the Black Lagoon*, *E.T.*, and *Neutral Spaces*), a full bar, a couple of stools and the exact same signage. Uncanny really and if it wasn't real, I'd say it was possible. Chris asks if we want to play pool and I decline in a way that attempts to downplay how fucking high I am, but probably is a dead give away. Tex and Chris play a couple of games while I look at my phone and watch apps wiggle. It's making me giggle. I try pinball, but they all say tilt and I give up as quickly as I start. I tell them I need to go to the bathroom and slip away to spoon some ketamine up my nose. Lights on in the bathroom I'm able to take inventory of the white ring around my nostril, and wash it away with soap and water. Return down the steps wobbling and wiggling and giggling and yet Tex and Chris are nowhere to be found, a backdoor left open that I follow through out of instinct and guiding sense of probably. Tex and Chris and bent over looking at something under high-power lamps.

CHRIS: Pretty nice, huh?

TEX: Hell yeah. How much is that you're growing?

CHRIS: Now? Just a couple of ounces. For my cult, y'know how it is. Got spores mail order and been on it since probably right after you left. All in, I've probably grown a QP.

TEX: Aw man, I would've loved if you had this while I was here. All you had was that gnarly weed.

CHRIS: Shrooms are so much easier to grow and it keeps all my followers in check. I got a batch for you if you're interested.

TEX: Yes. I'm sure Kurt will want some too.

Love being the drug guy until I'm the "drug guy." I'm more than the substances I consume. Sure my father did acid hundreds of time in the seventies and after I tried it for the first time I felt like I'd become to the person I'd always been destined to be and maybe I'd been part LSD this whole time and through the transitive property of semen was always meant to spend years at a time microdosing so not to be a depressed piece of shit that everyone else around me seems to be. That comes at a price though. Did he say cult? Soon people start thinking drugs are your only interest and become a bit patronizing, intentional or otherwise. Tex means best, but come on buddy.

Tex and Chris hug like old friends who don't know the next time they'll see each other. A firm one that says it might be the last so just in case, but not long enough that either of them start to feel overly uncomfortable. I wonder if they've ever hugged before. Doesn't look like it. In the car Tex shows me the mushrooms and asks if I want to take one and I laugh and say no way but offer no further explanation like I'm already fucking on one bro.

TEX: I think I'm gonna take one.
KURT: What?
TEX: Some mushrooms. Like a cap and a stem. I dunno. Make it interesting. See if I can keep it together in front of parents.
KURT: Uh—okay.

That sounds like a terrible idea and it definitely turns into one. Tex spends the evening crying and pacing in his childhood bedroom while I play Settlers of Catan with Mr. and Mrs. Gresham at the kitchen table. We eat Steak Tips (Medium Rare) for dinner. I find it unsettling that neither of them are willing to tell me their first names and demand to be addressed as Mr. and Mrs. Gresham. Conversation turns to the name of my book and I tell them that all I have is a temp title.

MR. GRESHAM: Well, what is it?
KURT: Modern Drugs Ain't So Hard to Find If You Know Where to Look.
MRS. GRESHAM: Oh.

Later in the evening we do karaoke. I do "Casey Jones" by the Dead. Mr. Gresham does "Long Train Runnin" by the Doobie Brothers. And Mrs. Gresham does an angry (and surprisingly direct) rendition of "Hit The Road Jack" by Ray Charles. Tex never leaves his room. I am still very high. At breakfast nobody addresses the night before.

TEX

There's an old desk in my old room where I scratched the word "booger" underneath. I'm on my back, on the floor, looking up at this word, tracing the etched letters with my finger. I did this. When I was like nine or ten. And it's still here. The word, the desk, this room—even though a stray cat lives here now. Like a literal stray, feral cat. Shits on all my old things. Found a huge turd in my autographed "Weird Al" hat.

Kurt knocks on the door again. Sometimes you have to leave.

So I say goodbye to my parents—Mr. & Mrs. Gresham. They cry. I want to but don't. They follow us out, stand by the front door, watching us drive away. It'll be another three or four years before we see each other again—maybe. Remember: I've been thinking of ending things.

KURT

What'd you say?

TEX

Nothing.

On the way out of the neighborhood where I grew up, we drive past the house where my friend Steven lived and he's out on the lawn with his dad. They're both tending to a garden that's overflowing with various colored flowers—marigolds and azaleas and hyacinths and sunflowers. A sign reads GARDEN OF THE MONTH. Kurt's driving so I keep my eyes on Steven and his dad, working away. Sweating with smiles. And as if in slow motion (and to the opening synth/ piano hits of The Who's "Baba O'Riley") Steven turns to me, still smiling, and waves—his smile like a supernova in the middle of his face. My hand lifts, but doesn't wave. Stuck. Can't move it.

And then we turn the corner and Steven's gone.

> KURT

Who was that?

> TEX

My friend. Steven.

> KURT

You wanna turn back? Say hey? We got time.

> TEX

No no no no… It's cool. Let's get on the road like Jack Kerowhack.

Kurt flips on the radio and puts the pedal to the metal, still in the neighborhood. I don't have the guts to tell him that Steven died in 2014—two months before his dad.

My phone buzzes—a DM from @melancory666 that reads: **heard you were talkin shit about kerouac. not on my watch, homie.** I look at Kurt, but his eyes are on the road.

Didn't have time to say anything online. Another DM comes in: **we're always listening, homie**. I throw my phone in the backseat.

Houston traffic is like the mine cart scene in *Indiana Jones and the Temple of Doom*. Meaning there's always a screaming woman in your car and weird thuggees trying to jump onto your car and rip your heart out. This all happens at about 120mph, because if you go any slower people will pull upside the car and blow out your tires with a .44 Magnum. The roadways are complex, old, and confusing. And the skyline feels like every skyscraper's ledge is adorned with that gargoyle gremlin from *Gremlins 2: The New Batch*.

In other words: I'm glad when it's in our rearview.

The main interstate that takes you from coast-to-coast (I-10) cuts through some depressingly rural and rundown towns in East Texas—and yeah, that's capital. East Texas is a whole other fucking planet.[4] And I kinda wanna show it to Kurt. So after Beaumont and the hella-racist territory known as Vidor, we hop onto HWY12, then FM105, then ride HWY96. I assure Kurt that 69 connects to 84, which will bring us into Louisiana, and 84 connects to 49 which is both the lot that cries and the highway that'll bring us to Baton Rouge and back to I-10. It's a loop that's so goddamn out of the way that it's completely not worth it—but it'll be interesting to see these places that ooze primordial poverty and maybe leave a copy or two of *Heck* in a

---

[4] I've written extensively about East Texas in my book *Heck, Texas* (published by Atlatl Press)—which I'm just now realizing we totally forgot to promote and sell any copies of while in Houston. Shit… On the way back— maybe.

random gas station.

When we pass the sign **Entering JASPER City Limits**, I turn to Kurt and go—

TEX
Oh, dude. Wait until you see this place. It's gnarly.

KURT
It's so empty out here.

I tell him to get off 96 so we can drive through Main Street, see the town and all that. There's bound to be some kind of historical marker of racism we can point at and go *Jesus Christ, this place is fucked up.*

But when we get to the town square, it's beautiful. Quaint small town center park with a gazebo in the middle, park ringed by small businesses and restaurants. Families walking hand-in-hand. And not just white families. Families of all colors. Peacefully coexisting, living the American dream. It's the kind of place I would move to and live if I didn't have the desperate need to be the center of attention and to live in a place that feels important or the center of cultural attention— even though I hate living in Las Vegas.

KURT
Didn't you write a book about how fucked up this place is?

TEX
Shut up.

                    KURT

It's, like, really nice.

                    TEX

I dunno, man. It's been like two decades since I
was last here. It changed.

                    KURT

Shit usually does.

                    TEX

The book's out. I can't do anything about it.

                    KURT

Who cares.

We stop at a Dairy Queen and get two peanut butter cup
Blizzards™—they turn it upside down and everything. We
swap seats—I drive and eat while Kurt eats and scrolls through
Twitter, no longer interested in the part of Texas I told him
would be fun in a fucked up way but which is just kinda boring
and calm and filled with mostly-empty cow pastures. We both
complain about how the dairy's gonna mess up our stomachs.

Then the rear driver's side tire pops somewhere on HWY84,
right outside of Joaquin. I mean, I know how to change a tire.
But I'm lazy as fuck and I'm tired and I've only got one pair of
pants—still—and I don't really want to get them dirty. Kurt
and I are about to paper-scissors-rock to see who changes it
when an old battered van pulls up. It's all rusted and boxy. It's
huge... and reminds me of something.

KURT

Dude… Look at the license plate.

It reads **BEATNGU** and again, I swear I recognize all of it from somewhere. The driver's door opens.

TEXAS BRO STRANGLER

I fixt them boys tire. Flat as a lot lizerds dignity, it was. Said theys driving to Florida and I told them they on the wrong road and the ugly one said theys was lookin at the towns round these parts and I dont know what to make of that. Aint nothin around here but cows and slaughterhouses and the Old Gods land. Aint like a New York City. But I could tell them boys was from California or one of them floaty places where they minds is all rotten. Knew they was gonna be my new meat treats moment I set my reptile eyes on them. Whiles I was fixin theys tire, somethin in they trunk kept a-goin thump a-thump. Poundin. The ugly one kept standin by the trunk like he was tryin to block it from me. Like theys got somethin in there. I gave them my devil grin. Same one I give all my meat treats. Make em not scared. The not ugly one tried to put five dollars in my hand and I spat on it. Disgusting. I aint a store. I aint to be bought. Once yous a meat treat yous always my meat treat. Them reptile eyes dont look away. I went back to my truck to get the rope and the cattle blaster and the poison and the acid juice and the skeleton dagger and the flesh book and the naked bone cage. But when I getted back them boys was already in they car driving away without their flat tire or theys tire iron or theys car jack. But the reptile eyes was on them hard and so I getted back in my truck and take the tire and iron and jack and let the hellhounds get they scent. And I follow them. My new meat treats. They head east. Aint no one around and I put the pedal to the floor and the devils engine screams and the truck blasts onward. Hunting them. And I almost getted them but they drive like reckless madmen and getted to the old Crossing Bridge before I catch them and they cross the Ancient River into Louisiana Territory and I aint following them over there cuz thats the Swamp Venom Queen's land and all the meat treats belong to her there. I turn back and the reptile eyes put theyselves on a car of bro faces as they pass over the Crossing Bridge into Texas Land and head west. My new meat treats. Yum yum.

- LOUISIANA -

KURT

There's a Barnes & Noble in Lafayette and another one in Baton Rouge. Three in the general vicinity of New Orleans. We've got a trunk full of books and nowhere for them to go. Truth is Tex paid $3000+ to have his book published, and while the publishing house sent him 300 copies, he'd have to sell each one for at least $10 to cut even. So far he'd sold 112 which was paltry in comparison to Dan Brown standards but better than F. Scott Fitzgerald ever did in his lifetime. Eight boxes stacked in his parking space back in Las Vegas, two in our trunk and we hadn't sold a single one on the ride out here. Big plans to stop at every independent bookstore this side of the Mississippi (and the other side too) to try and take some copies for—fuck, what's that word where they sell the book for you and give you a cut of the money?—consignment.

The plan was flawed from the beginning as the way to do this was probably drive north from San Diego instead of West. Hit Verbatim in San Diego. The Last Bookstore and Skylight Books in Los Angeles. The Henry Miller Library in Big Sur. Probably half a dozen spots in San Francisco. At least Powell's in Portland and I'm sure somewhere in Seattle, but I've never been so I don't know for certain. Kris? In the age of the e-reader and the death of the death of the death of the novel (for more see Jessica Pressman's *Bookishness*) the word had come on down from high (the stock market) that Barnes & Noble was now an independent bookseller and must act accordingly.

We sit in the parking lot of the Lafayette Barnes & Noble. Next to a Best Buy and across the street from a Bed, Beth & Beyond, the green letters loom over Tex's white car and it doesn't feel very independent. Maybe more like Independent music when Alternative had worn it's welcome and critics needed a different way to refer to Death Cab For Cutie than they did Soundgarden. Independent like that. Independent like the local credit union aka still a fucking bank. Tex nervously rifles through the books in his box.

TEX: What if they don't take them
KURT: They probably won't.
TEX: Then what are we doing here?
KURT: Let's just go in and put like two or three copies on the shelf. Sneak em in.
TEX: Yeah, I mean, I don't care about the money.
KURT: What's $20 bucks?
TEX: A Blu-Ray copy of *Color of Money*.
KURT: See if they'll trade for it?
TEX: You think?

But he can tell from the look on my face that I don't think. We stuff copies into whatever pockets they'll fit into and head into the once corporate behemoth that looks downright downtrodden next to quadrillionaire Jeff Bezos's Amazon.com. I've heard rumors that the Amazon algorithm reads your book and if you say negative things about them or the guy in charge that they won't run your book. So let me just say up front that I love the guy and that in no way is he partially responsible for the downfall of America.

Inside, Barnes & Noble looks like the end of retail as we know it. Not a single customer in sight, dust on the shelves, two employees in matching green vests—one named Rupert and the other named Rupricht—raise their heads from mid-afternoon naps with a desperate smile that screams please buy something sirs. Anything. Can we interest you in our vast array of Funko Pop vinyl figurines?

Quickly find the Experimental Narrative section and make room for two copies of *Heck, Texas* between the works of Eckhard Gerdes and John Hawkes. It looks nice so we snap a photograph, only in that moment realizing that we probably should have recorded it. Put fools on a fool's errand and things don't even get done. Make a quick plan to double back and do it over but stop when we realize that Rupert and Rupricht have us cornered closing down the aisle. Okay, okay, back up slowly. I don't think they know what we've done, each one holding a Funko pop with a lurid look in their eye, repeating the phrase ENH? As if that's any kind of sales tactic at all. Out of mostly a sense of guilt Tex buys that copy of *Color of Money* and I, a Hunter S. Thompson Funko Pop. Keep this independent business afloat for another month.

In Baton Rouge, things feel a little less desperate, so we stock our pockets up with copies of Tex's book that will never sell and head inside only to find the situation eerily familiar. Replace dust with cobwebs and the rup/ert/richt twins with an automated computer salesman named B.A.R.N.E.S.Y..

B.A.R.N.E.S.Y.: Hello [PAUSE] KKUURRTT and [PAUSE] TEX, what can I help you with today?

TEX: This is too fucking weird, I'm out.
KURT: No, wait.

Tex is already out the automated doors, B.A.R.N.E.S.Y. wishing him a nice day and extending an invitation to come back anytime. The robot and I have a standoff where it tries to guess what I'm looking for based on my barnesandnoble.com purchasing history (which is none) and ends up trying to figure it out based on my looks.

B.A.R.N.E.S.Y.: Would you like me to direct you to the [pause] Fantasy section?
KURT: Oh no thanks, I just kind of want to look around.
B.A.R.N.E.S.Y.: You look like a [pause] Graphic Novel kind of [pause] dude.
KURT: Do you have any Sam Pink novels?
B.A.R.N.E.S.Y.: [pause] Sam Pink? Sam Pink? Hmmm… We have a book on cooking Salmon until it is no longer Pink. Is this what you would like to see?
KURT: I'm gonna just—

I don't even finish my thought, instead weaving my way down the rows and between shelves in a way that I believe would be most challenging for a Robot to keep up with, losing him on a couple of complicated turns and ducking low so his all-seeing webcam eyes can't spot my head sticking out from across the other side of the store. There is no EXPERIMENTAL FICTION section here, so I settle for CYBERWRITING. Take out my camera and flip to the front-facing one. Regular Michael Moore, pushing the documentary narrative to serve my needs when a robotic claw grabs my wrist and says:

B.A.R.N.E.S.Y.: Your move, creep.

I try to explain to the officers as they place me in the back of their cruiser that I was putting a book on the shelf instead of stealing one, but they're not buying it. Hope that Tex follows me to the station, but I look out the back window and don't see any familiar cars trailing after us.

By the time we make it to New Orleans we've given up the dream.

TEX

I call the hospital and then about forty-nine minutes into the on-hold jazz I realize Kurt's not in the hospital. He's in jail. So I call the jail and a woman who sounds like she's eating crackers and smoking Parliaments tells me *He ain't in the system yet* and hangs up on me without telling me exactly when to call back. So I start calling every twenty to twenty-five minutes.

I assume bail for sneaking books into a Barnes & Noble can't be too much. I've got cash—probably enough for whatever it is.

I lose trace of how many times I call, but eventually Lady Parliaments tells me that *Mr. RRTT's bail is set at $25,000* and when I say *What the fuck? For sticking books in Barnes & Noble?* she says *The charges are as follows* and she lists all these things that sound really really bad. Like attempted deactivation of a consumer-assistance droid, attempted product fraud, and falsifying information to an officer. And then she hangs up on me again.

Make a call to bail bondsman because I think that's what I'm supposed to do, dude named Max Strawberry. Tells me that a $25,000 bail requires a payment of $2,500 with a fee of $500 and that since *Mr. RRTT was remitted to the Barton Rouge Central Jail after 5pm, bail cannot be posted until after 8am tomorrow.* And I'm like *Fuck that*. It's my turn to hang up on someone.

I've got an idea.

Go to some fancy suit store and spend about $1,300 on a suit, dress shirt, tie, and slick wingtips. It's a little tight, but I don't have time to get it tailored. Next stop: a military surplus store. They sell badges, badge holders, and things like that. Get the idea? I'm gonna bust into that fucking police station tomorrow like I'm an FBI agent, tell them Kurt's to be remitted into my custody for questioning on interstate charges, and spring that motherfucker. Look, it's crazy, yeah… But, like, what else in this whole stupid journey hasn't been? Besides, I probably won't be around long enough to get in trouble for it.

But I gotta wait until tomorrow.

Find somewhere to sleep. There's a hotel. Big dark towering thing that's like five minutes from the jail. Hôtel Trou Du Cul Pourri in flickering hot pink neon. From the outside, it looks mostly abandoned. A few boarded up windows. But whatever. I don't care. There are cars in the parking lot. I park next to something from the 70s that's missing two tires and a back window.

But the inside is fucking unreal. Looks like the Gold Room from *The Shining* when it's in full bloom—but, like, without the people. It just looks nice. Place is still empty. Whatever.

But behind the counter, like a mirage or like a hallucination is someone I recognize and refuse to believe is truly there because I haven't talked to him in over ten years. Short-cropped gray hair, big serial killer glasses, nametag on his pink blazer that reads **Donald**. I walk up, dressed in my new sharp suit, like I'm supposed to be here.

                    TEX
Donald... What... What are you doing here?

                    DONALD
Can I help you?

                    TEX
It's Tex... Your twin brother?

                    DONALD
Oh... Yeah. Right. I own this place now.

                    TEX
Why?

                    DONALD
It's haunted.

                    TEX
                (laughing)
Yeah, right.

                    DONALD
No, dude. It's fucking haunted.

                    TEX
Oh... I guess I'll take a room then.

He gives me the key to Room 49—an actual key, not a keycard. I pay. Whatever. Regular hotel shit. And I go to the elevators, which are out of order. So I have to take the stairs.

And the second I open the door to the stairwell, things suck.

Rats pour out and the grounds overflowing with some kind of chunky water. There's trash everywhere. Pieces of building float in the water. I go back to the entrance, to the reception, but it's different. Like old looking. Spiderwebs and broken shit. Furniture's all half-burnt. And Donald's gone. In his place is a mannequin with a smashed-in head.

This is normal, I guess.

I wade through the water, and start my climb up stairs that feel tiled, as if the entire building itself is leaning heavily in one direction. Embers fall from far above, float down and wisp around in unfelt wind. A steady *thump* of some kind of tribal drum reverberates through the building.

Room 49 is on the 19th floor—if that makes sense. The room's at the end of a long hallway that looks like the aftermath of a warzone. The floor's squishy with something red and sticky. All the doors are broken down, looking in on rooms mostly black—except for a faint red flickering light. Like embers roaming the room's emptiness. Room 49 is the only room with a door still attached.

I enter. It's a nice room. A bed. A toilet. A window that looks out on a red skied night. Whatever. I'm only sleeping here.

I set an alarm on my phone to wake up early and go get Kurt. I wonder what he's doing, if he's okay. I'm sure he is. I wouldn't be, but he's the kind of guy who could make friendly with anyone. He'd be great in marketing, but that kinda work goes against his nature.

I get in bed, still in my suit.

I've got enough time in this hotel room to think and let the depression sink in more and realize all the reasons why I feel angry and sad and disappointed. I want too much, I guess. I hoped for more than what I am right now. Everyone's like this, but it weighs heavier on others—I'm one of these others, I guess. I work and I write and it all feels for nothing. I enjoy doing it, but anyone who says they write and create for themselves and not for an audience is a liar trying to make themselves feel better by lying to themselves, denying that little voice that's always cawing like a raven in the back of their head, saying *Respect me respect me.* All I want is for people to like me like I like people. I don't want to feel like the things I do are totally pointless. I feel cursed. Like I'm being followed around by a ghost who keeps shitting on me over and over. I want respect. I want to be important and not just some guy out here grasping at nothing. And I don't care who—could be someone in Arkansas or Greenland or fucking Romania or some shit. I just want to feel like the things I do mean more than just things I do. I want to be more than just—

GHOST IN THE CORNER OF THE ROOM
Please shut the fuck up!

                        TEX
        Sorry…

I roll over and go to bed. The ghost in the corner of the room
turns on the TV to an episode of *Home Improvement* and laughs
louder than the laugh track every time Tim "The Tool Man"
Taylor fucks something up. I don't remember there being a TV
in the room.

            TIM "THE TOOL MAN" TAYLOR
            More power! Argh argh argh!

        GHOST IN THE CORNER OF THE ROOM
            Yo, you mind if I rub one out?

                        TEX
        …go for it.

I fall asleep to the sounds of sitcom laughter and ectoplasmic
slapping.

When I wake up the ghost is gone. There's no TV. Everything
about the room is normal. I've sweated through the suit. It's all
wrinkled. Must've tossed all night. I get up, slap cool water on
my face. Leave. No trash in the halls. No cobwebs. No floating
embers. It's all just basic and old. Donald nods a goodbye like
he doesn't know me as I set the room key on the counter on
my way out. Guess I just stayed in a shitty motel for the night.
Guess I used a bit of imagination or something. Guess I'm
bored. Guess the Great American Roadtrip ain't as great as I
thought it'd be. Oh well… Shit.

KURT

The holidays are full of tradition. And that doesn't change just because I'm in a Baton Rouge jail cell. Officer Lewinson brings in a plate of Christmas Ham for each of us, slathered in pineapple juice and walnuts. We eat until we're stuffed and have to unbutton our pants just to make room for seconds. They took our belts away otherwise we'd certainly be undoing those as well. It's honestly the best ham I've ever eaten but the Officers on the other side of the bars swear it's just from the counter at Calandro's Supermarket. Don't push the issue any further after the third or fourth time I ask because the officers get testy and threaten to not give us dessert.

Slice of pecan pie and we're onto the white elephant exchange. They've wrapped things found in the evidence locker. The paper has beavers in christmas hats and lights strung over wooden dams and I've never been so grateful for anybody in my entire life. The thought and care that went into making it a special day for Bobby, Phil, and me.

PHIL: It's I. "Bobby, Phil, and" I.
KURT: Oh, my bad.
PHIL: We all make mistakes.
KURT: Do you actually think you could copy edit this book for me?
PHIL: Yeah, email it to me.

KURT: I will when I get my phone back.

And we have a laugh. Solid guys, Bobby and Phil. Sure Bobby is here for B&E, but he was just trying to steal his kid a Nintendo Switch for the holidays and who can blame him for that. Phil won't tell us what he's in for, but every time we ask he starts to giggle uncontrollably. The kind of laugh that's really infectious. That you just want to join in on and laugh too. Have it out, slapping the knee like a banjo player down south in the swamps. In the white elephant I end up with Bobby's gun and he ends up with Phil's Human Skull. Phil ends up with my ketamine. We all switch, satisfied with what was already ours.

We end up doing some drugs to pass the night, singing Christmas Carols as best we're able under the influence. They tell me that it's Joyeux Noël in French and I tell them that I'm learning German but don't know what the translation is. We all agree that it's the best Christmas we've ever had and vow to meet up again every year (but maybe not in the same place). The officers share their rum-spiked eggnog with us and come morning we're all in matching police issue jammies watching that fucking movie where the kid shoots his eye out. Once the sun crests over the horizon, Officer Lewison unlocks the door and opens it wide.

OFFICER LEWISON: Here's a Christmas Miracle. We're dropping all your charges. In the spirit of the season. Since you're such good guys and all.
BOBBY: Oh wow, that's so kind of you.
PHIL: Thank you Satan. I mean Santa.
KURT: Really appreciate this. Let me get your address.

Definitely sending you a Christmas card next year.

I do too. Send Officer Jack Lewison a christmas card up until the year 2047 where paper is banned. Would send him an ecard, but never get his email address. Sometimes it feels like you can know someone so well and never even follow them on Instagram. Bobby and Phil ask if I want a ride anywhere but I politely decline as I've got a Florida to get to. They both ask, 'ew, why?' and I say I'm not so sure anymore.

TEX

I'm on the way to the jail, ready to be… Agent Stephanie Johnson? Shit! I realize the badge I bought is for a woman… Fuck, I don't know. I guess I can still pull it off. People will question it less, right? Not PC to go *Yeah, but you're a man*. It's perfect. But then my phone rings. I answer.

KURT
They let me out. Come pick me up?

TEX
Fuck… All right.

And now I'm wearing this suit for no reason. Not just wearing it, but bought it. Damn. I could probably return it.

I grab some coffee on the way there cuz I'm sure Kurt hasn't had any all night. He's probably hungry too. I snatch up some jelly-filled donuts, four breakfast sandwiches and like six hashbrowns from Lucy In The Sky With Donuts.

The bedraggled Kurt I imagine isn't the one I pick up. He looks well-rested, well-fed. Happy even. Happier than he's been this whole trip. He even gives me a double thumbs up and skips the rest of the way to the car.

TEX

I got some food and coffee.

KURT

Oh I'm not hungry. But thanks for the coffee.

He offers to drive while I eat, but I like eating and driving. Especially in places I've never been. I ask how it was and he just shrugs. There's no way he's hiding some traumatic event behind this facade of positivity, right? Either way, I'm not gonna ask.

KURT

Thanks for getting me.

TEX

Yeah, sorry. Couldn't bail you out until the morning.

KURT

Nice suit.

TEX

Thanks.

KURT

What'd you do last night?

TEX

Uh…

I want to show him the hotel where I stayed last night, but

when we drive by where it's supposed to be the only thing there is an empty, swampy lot. I could be wrong about where it's supposed to be, but I know I'm not. It's gone. Vanished. Like it never existed.

Now we both have things we don't want to talk about.

I want to do something before we leave because I feel like the trip's going too fast. There are signs for a Swamp Nature Center and when I point it out, Kurt gives a moderately enthused nod. So we follow the signs and end up at this well-maintained system of trails that radiate from a Jurassic-Park-like visitor center and out into a thick buzzing swamp. We don't get a map. We just start walking.

Neither of us speak as we take in the coldly humid surrounding. Splashes in the water as gators and red-eared turtles dive out of our view. Birds screech and chirp from every limb. There's black windows and gray wolf spiders proudly displaying their fishing-line-thick webs, knowing they'll be there for years, undisturbed. We take a moment at a lookout point, take in the Louisiana swamp that looks like a stock photo titled *Louisiana Swamp*.

TEX
(doing a very bad Werner Herzog
impression)

The trees here are in misery, and the birds are in misery.

KURT
That from *Terminator*?

TEX
Total Recall.

I half expect us to see Bigfoot or Swamp Ape or a couple of French gangsters dumping a body in the gator infested water. But this ain't like that.

The tour of the swamp ends with some Cajun-sounding guy giving us whole raw chickens, tells us to feed the gators—which are dangerously close to the shore and there's nothing protecting us from them. Kurt tosses his chicken and the gators lunge out of the water, fighting over the raw meat. It's manic and primal. Pure animal rage and instinct. Two fight over the chicken, rip it in half and choke down the halves. And before I can toss my chicken in the water, a woman wearing a polo embroidered with the Reserve's name hurries over, stops me, and grabs the man who gave us the chickens.

WOMAN WHO WORKS AT RESERVE
Goddammit, Fontenot. How many times do we have to tell you? You can't feed the gators!

CAJUN GUY
E'skiddle e'o'doe.

She takes him away. He rambles, pointing at me. I toss the chicken in the water and the Cajun guy claps and laughs as the gators tear the chicken apart.

We get back in the car and start off for the last Act of the tour. Florida almost upon us. And then it hits me: Shit… I forgot to return the suit.

CAVIN FUCKING GONZALEZ

Ketamine ketamine ketamine.

What *is* ketamine?

GOOGLE SEARCH: What is ketamine?

GOOGLE RESULT: *"Ketamine, categorized as a 'dissociative anesthetic,' is used in powdered or liquid form as an anesthetic, usually on animals. It can be injected, consumed in drinks, snorted, or added to joints or cigarettes. Ketamine was placed on the list of controlled substances in the US in 1999. Short- and long-term effects include increased heart rate and blood pressure, nausea, vomiting, numbness, depression, amnesia, hallucinations and potentially fatal respiratory problems. Ketamine users can also develop cravings for the drug. At high doses, users experience an effect referred to as 'K-Hole,' an 'out of body' or 'near-death' experience."*

Hm. Okay. I have done DMT exactly one time. DMT was analgesic in that it forced me, quite literally, into my bed where it took over my mind. David Bowie was playing over my computer and my room was pitch black. Lasers crept in from my periphery and began morphing across the walls like a fucking 80s Zepplin laser show you'd see depicted in cartoons —the kind of scene where, were you a drug user, you'd think: "Ah! Drugs aren't like that!"

DMT was like that.

DMT was, in every way, quite abysmal of an experience. The visuals were quite nice. But there was a… creeping physicality to the experience which began in my toes. I felt a slight pressure building in my toes from the moment I face planted into my bed. It crept up and up, growing stronger, more pronounced, and this experience could best be described as sleep paralysis. Like a sleep paralysis demon… creeping up your body. And the visuals were growing more erratic and pronounced as well, as the pressure moved from my toes to up my torso and finally into my chest—my heart—and once I felt the compression on my chest I thought to myself: "One day I am going to die… and it will feel like this" which immediately frightened me. I moved my hands to my wrist to check for a pulse and found none. I put my fingers to my ribcage and was certain my heart had stopped. Bowie laughed from the computer speakers and geometric designs descended from the walls and ceiling down unto my eyes, filling my skull with hectic lights and flashes of images too violent and horrible to describe here.

I mark this DMT trip as "the descent."

I have been trying to "ascend" ever since.

You might think it is counterintuitive to combat mental fatigue and illness spurred by illegal drug consumption by introducing yet another psycho-active compound to one's psyche and, naturally, you would be right.

Doesn't matter if you're right, though.

Haha—fuck you.

Understand?

GOOGLE SEARCH: *ketamine and depression*

GOOGLE RESULT: *"At lower doses, it can help ease pain. Ketamine helps sedatives work and may help people need fewer addictive painkillers, like morphine after surgery or while caring for burns..."*

Hm.

I feel around my body: touching my toes, feets, legs, chest, and skull. I reach in through my nose, digging quite deep, and place a cool hand around the base of my brain. I am looking for pain. I find it, oh yes, so much. So much pain!

GOOGLE RESULT [CONTINUED]: *"Outside of the clinic, ketamine can cause tragedies, but in the right hands, it is a miracle,' says John Abenstein, MD, president of the American Society of Anesthesiologists..."*

DM to KKUURRTT: Are you trying to cause a tragedy?

DM from KKUURRTT: This is a comedy.

DM to KKUURRTT: Ur positive?

DM from KKUURRTT: For several schedule 1 substances. And schedule 2. Maybe 3.

GOOGLE RESULT [CONTINUED (part 2)]: *Researchers are studying whether ketamine can help treat severe depression, such as in people who have tried other treatments or who are in the hospital and possibly suicidal. The FDA hasn't approved it for that use. But some psychiatrists are trying ketamine experimentally with their patients who have this type of depression, says John Krystal, MD, chief of psychiatry at Yale-New Haven Hospital. People usually take antidepressants for a few weeks before they start to work. Those medicines need to build up in your system to have an effect. Ketamine is different. Its effects on depression happen as it leaves your body, Krystal says.*

Researchers aren't sure exactly why that is. One theory is that ketamine prompts connections to regrow between brain cells that are involved in mood. Krystal calls the effect "profound" and says the drug works "far more rapidly" than today's antidepressant pills.

Okay.

Enough is enough, and this is enough.

I have read enough. Learned enough. Seen enough.

Ketamine: *the answer.*

Yes… yes yes yes.

Of course.

DM to KKUURRTT: Where r u guys

DM from KKUURRTT: this is a cop lol ur friend is in jail. it's ok tho. we fed him Gud

DM to KKUURRTT: lol ok but do u have the ketamine? i'd really like to do the ketamine, of which i mean the illicit, illegal substance you are trafficking across several state lines. please. i need help..

Radio silence.

DM to KKUURRTT: Fuck 12—suck a dick!

Radio silence.

KURT

Crawdad Po'Boys. Strolling the French Quarter. Listening to some Jazz. Saying "I like this" and Tex saying "I like this too." Agreeing for the rest of the road trip to only listen to Jazz music. Realizing we don't know many Jazzists and spending the next 5 to 10 minutes looking at our phone typing in different variations of COOL JAZZ and EXPERIMENTAL JAZZ and TOP TEN JAZZ ARTISTS THAT INTERESTING PEOPLE LIKE into our search bars (Tex uses Bing—"that's BING baby"). Admiring the architecture. Doing acid (again?) in a cemetery and recreating that sequence in *Easy Rider* shot for shot (who knew this title would pay off?) adding in the lens flares and 16mm grain in post. Spending 7 hours in a coffee shop staring at Tex's laptop as he crafts it into a video and I drink coffee. Uploading the video to Twitter and skipping right past Youtube. Getting seven likes each and being satisfied with that. Trying to talk in Louisiana accents and getting annoyed looks from the people passing us by in the streets. Mardi Grasing.

We end up on a tour van that takes you to sites devastated by Hurricane Katrina, and stand in the bad part of town and look at dilapidated buildings that have stood ignored and water-logged for fifteen years, wondering if they'll ever turn this area around sure doesn't seem like it and think about how this was somebody's home and it all just feels so grim when we really stop and take a moment to think about it. After the second stop we ask the driver to take us back to the fun stuff because this is, and I quote, depressing. He does and we tip him an extra $5 for the trouble and he tells us it happens all the time. Tells us that the tour ends at the abandoned Six Flags and we're bitter that we didn't stick it through.

Climb out in front of a voodoo & beignet shop entitled Voodoo & Beignet Shoppe. At the front counter, we both buy beignets, letting powdered sugar fall to the carpet with abandon while we peruse the aisles for something we can bring home to our significant others. I get Lauren a blessed chicken foot (purple) and Tex gets V a tank top (red), both agreeing that they'll be disappointed with our purchases but not really inspired by anything else on the shelves. See a sign that says "CUSTOM VOODOO DOLLS" and each get one made of the other. Take turns flicking the crotch and bringing each other to their knees. Just like that Jackass show. After about three hits we decide to truce and throw the dolls in the trash— truly where we belong.

In the corner sits a woman at a small table, beckoning us with her eyes. The kind of look across a room that is a tractor beam of this is where you belong, come to me my two scared men. We take a seat, and both pull a $20 out of our wallet for a tarot reading as if mesmerized into it and money is no option. Madame Space asks us questions, but we refuse to answer anything, zipping our lips so she has to do all the work without the assistance of information. She spreads her deck and pulls JUDGEMENT and THE TOWER and THREE OF SWORDS and proceeds to explain that this tells her that we're on the wrong path for what we're looking for.

Get a second po'boy: this time with shrimp. Much better than the crawdad one. Or maybe we just went to a better spot this go around. We'll never know. On Frenchmen Street instead of Bourbon Street. They're playing Jazz there too. Lick our lips and fingertips. Feel like tourists. Such a cliché.

- MISSISSIPPI -

TEX

Tomorrow, we're going to Florida. But tonight, we're playing poker with a bunch of Bible salesmen in Mississippi. Found them in a neighborhood when Kurt had the brilliant idea of trying to sell copies of *Heck, Texas* door-to-door. Run into one of the salesmen, goes by the name Rabbit. He comments on my suit. And when he sees I'm not selling bibles, but instead some kind of demonic text with the work "heck" on the cover, we decide to team up. Kurt and I go in, acting like satanic assholes—someone buys *Heck*, cool. They never do. And then Rabbit comes in with the bible, saving the lone housewife or the day-drunk retiree from certain damnation from having interacted with Kurt and I. Rabbit gives us a small cut of his commission. Seems like legit work. I only play six hands of poker before I'm too tired. I fall asleep in the only bed in the room. I lose $500 and Kurt wins $12.

- ALABAMA -

KURT

UHHHHH... who gives a shit? Road is road. Tex drives 110 the whole way and we make it through Alabama in less than 30 mins, stateline to stateline, even though it should be more than double that if you're following signs that say otherwise. Nothing to report, so I won't. We set up the camera on the dashboard to film us as we drive through but the camera falls forward and ends up filming the center console and we don't notice until we cross into Florida. Get really into Sun Ra Arkestra, headbanging in unison to psychedelic time signatures and aggressive dissonance. Jazz, baby.

- BUCHAREST -

TOBIAS

Intrăm în București pe la opt noaptea. Ridic coletul de la poștal. Este mic și ștampilat cu multe sigilii de la departamentul de securitate - atât român, cât și american. Nu aștept până sunt acasă să-l deschid, așa că îl deschid în mașina lui Krisztian. Este cartea - un exemplar din *Heck, Texas* pe care l-am comandat de la un vânzător privat din America. Amazon nu va expedia cartea aici, așa că am avut un prieten pe nume Dave să cumpere o copie și să mi-o trimită prin poștă. O răsfoiesc și văd o poză cu o femeie cu fundul pentru față și caca pentru nas. Asta mă face să râd. Îi arăt lui Krisztian și râde și el. El pornește mașina și ne întoarcem în sat.

Satul nostru este mic, dar avem internet. Există clădiri care au fost dezvoltate în anii 1960, dar nu au fost niciodată finalizate. La ultimul etaj al celei mai înalte clădiri din satul nostru - am făcut un mic studio în care lucrăm eu și Krisztian. Scriem povești și scenarii. Lucrăm la o emisiune de televiziune despre un actor care dorește să fie faimos și se transformă într-un iepuraș de desene animate. Așa vom deveni celebri precum Text Greshan și KKUURRTT. Sunt cei mai cunoscuți scriitori din satul nostru. Toată lumea are o poză cu ei în casele lor. Ascultăm podcastul lor ON THEE ROAD noaptea - chiar dacă este doar episodul unic. Ne dau speranță. Pentru că dacă doi bărbați neglijenti ca Text și KKUURRTT pot fi iubiți de atât de mulți, atunci și Krisztian și cu mine putem. Cea mai mare parte a feței mele lipsește. Tatăl meu a tăiat-o cu un topor într-o noapte, în timp ce era beat. A crezut că sunt unchiul său mort și a continuat să strige „Nu mă vei întoarce înapoi în lemn, Geppetto!" Am învățat să trăiesc cu jumătate de chip. M-am născut cu un stomac pe exteriorul corpului meu. Krisztian nici măcar nu este om. Este un porc cu creier uman. Sper că într-o bună zi voi fi la fel de deștept ca el.

Suntem, de asemenea, mari fani ai lui Bud Smith. Dar noi îl numim Butt Smith.[5]

---

[5] Translation in appendix.

- FLORIDA -

<u>TEX</u>

We stop at a Burger King soon after crossing into Florida. It's off the highway in Pensacola. Kurt's not really hungry but I'm like ravenous for something sloppy and depressing. Burger King is always going to be that for me. The Whopper™ used to be something flat and sloppy and satisfying in a primitive way, but now they've tried to church it up and it's just sad. But still, I want one.

KURT
I'm gonna chill in the car.

TEX
Okay.

KURT
But get me a coffee. And some of those chicken fries.

TEX
Breakfast of champions.

KURT
Vurt Konnegu—

I slam the door.

You[6] ever been to Pensacola? If **No**—cool, don't go. If **Yes**— the beaches are beautiful but I hate where you live and it's all because of this Burger King.

So I go into the Burger King and it's mostly empty. There's one old man chomping on a kid's meal with a mouthful of gums. He looks like everyone's grandpa. I'd kinda like to order and go sit with him and eat and talk about stuff—see what all the old bastard's gone through in life. Leave Kurt out there a little bit. Put some space and time between us before the final stretch to Orlando.

But I don't do shit like that. I go up to the counter, order from a girl with a nametag that says **Burger** who doesn't respond when I say *Whopper*™ *with cheese (hold the tomatoes and lettuce), two large coffees, Chicken Fries*™*, and an order of fried Mac N' Cheetos*™*.* She only responds with the total. I pay and wait.

Ten minutes later—

BURGER
Here's ya order.

I don't bother thanking her cuz she clearly doesn't give a shit. But I check the order. Two coffees, Chicken Fries™, Mac N' Cheetos™, and the Whopper™ with cheese, hold the tomatoes and— Wait a goddamn second. There's tomatoes and lettuce on this bitch.

---

[6] I don't know who you are. But you're obviously someone—otherwise this and the I and the Kurt within this narrative wouldn't exist. So thank you for existing so that we can—for now.

> TEX

Excuse me.

> BURGER

What.

> TEX

There's tomatoes and lettuce on this. Can I get it without?

She grabs the burger from me, shuffles to the kitchen, slams the burger down and says *Y'all fuckin' up his order.* The kitchen's full of dudes and dudettes who remind me of the whitetrash kids from highschool who hung out behind the t-buildings and smoked cigars and stomped on frogs. They do something to the burger and she comes back with it and puts it on the counter without a word.

I check it. And somehow these motherfuckers took the goddamn cheese off it. I slide it back across.

> TEX

There's supposed to be cheese.

> BURGER

Jesus Christ.

She takes the burger back, they do their thing, and she comes back and slides it across again. I check it. There's cheese. But the tomatoes back and the fucking things a chicken sandwich now. I slide it back.

TEX

Just gimme a fuckin Whopper™ with cheese and keep the tomatoes and lettuce off it.

BURGER

What the hell's ™?

She takes the chicken sandwich. The kitchen people mess around for too long. And she comes back, hopefully for the final time, with the burger. I check it. Cheese, no tomatoes, no lettuce, and no fucking meat patty. And the amount of mayo they've slopped on it is criminal in 23 countries.

I take the burger and slam it on the counter. Mayo spurts everywhere like the end of a porn. I toss the burger at the kitchen people.

TEX

Fuck you, you motherfuckers!

They start coming for me. All of them. I toss the bag of food and the two coffees. Everything explodes against the machines and the walls. Dudes have their fists up, ready. And mine are ready to retaliate. And then this big, Dave Bautista looking dude emerges from the back like a nightmare and everyone points at me. I smile and bolt out of the Burger King.

I jump in the car right as Kurt ends a call and looks at the mayo all over my shirt. We haul ass out of the parking lot but get stuck at the stoplight right outside the Burger King. The workers stand at the door, flipping me the bird, shouting things I can't hear. Dave Bautista stares me down, daring me to come back. But they don't come after us—which is good.

Then a yellow '95 Mustang pulls up to the light next to us, windows rolled down, "I'm Just A Kid" by Simple Plan blaring from the stereo.

GUY IN YELLOW MUSTANG
Yo, bitch! Wanna race?

Kurt and I look at the guy in the Mustang, banging his head to the music, staring at us. Dude looks like a cross between Eminem and Jon Lovitz. Kurt and I both laugh at the same time. This pisses the guy off. His face turns sour and he whips out a handgun that looks like it's out of *The Fifth Element*. Points it at both of us. I wince, preparing to be shot in the face.

The guy laughs, peels out, and blasts through the red light—his cackle sounds like an ancient witch drifting off into the night. Cars that have the right of way slam on their brakes. We wait for the light to turn green.

Back on I-10, the Burger King five minutes in our past—

KURT
Did you get my Chicken Fries™?

CAVIN FUCKING GONZALEZ
AND THE WORST DAY EVER

Have you ever had a dream so profoundly mundane that the effect it had on you was much more pronounced than the most horrific, surreal torture your subconscious could possibly conjure?

Oh.

Yes...

Last night I had a dream that I bumped into my ex-girlfriend at the supermarket. We made small talk. The scenery drifted lazily; a park, a car, a restaurant, the sidewalk, finally—my bed.

It wasn't a sex dream. It was much worse. We were simply talking.

And smiling.

And laughing.

And when I woke up there was a murderous rage welling already.

A rage so murderous, in fact, that I could only cry in response.

Because it wasn't a rage at all. More like a passive, slow, longing... a realization that the past could be recaptured and a realization that the past could never, would never, ever, be recaptured.

There is only today, tomorrow.

And that person you once were, with that person who once was?

Dead, murdered in cold blood.

The both of you.

Dead, a twitching corpse of a union.

So I fingered about the bedside drawer for my anxiety medication and found the bottle and it was empty.

I fingered about for my SSRI's too and found the bottle and it was empty.

No more refills.

No more health insurance.

It was hailing outside. Hailing in the humid, muggy summer like some sick fucking joke.

God is a sadistic motherfucker.

A Floridian to be struck in the face by hail?

Yes, I believe in God.

I believe God is cruel and, specifically, has an interest in puppeting my life in a way that emulates some sadistic dark comedy.

Existing as a pun is no easy feat.

I ran through the hail and got to my car and drove off only to realize that I had forgotten my headphones, which are necessary for my job, and so I did a skidding U-turn and lurched into my driveway and again ran out into the hail/rain and into my house and obtained the item and…

Drove off only to realize that I had forgotten my wallet, which contains my ID, which is necessary for my job, and so I did a skidding U-turn and lurched into my driveway and again ran out into the hail/rain and into my house and obtained the item and:…

I was soaking fucking wet and my headlights were broken and my windshield wipers were broken and my front bumper was falling off my car, I could hear it scraping the road as I nervously drove towards my office.

Oh, yes!

Yes!

Fuck oh MY FUCKING GOD—and I forgot my umbrella. Which is why I was soaking wet.

Trudged through the mud and hail and rain completely drenched, soaking, sopping wet, and into the sub zero biome of The Office.

Once inside of The Office I looked around and felt, so certainly, as my eye twitched, and fists curled, and brain shouted, and skin screamed, and brain lashed out angrily like a fucking starving wolf that if I stayed...I tried to behave normally... a great, horrible event would unfold.

My boss approached me timidly, saw my state, and went to turn around.

"No," I said, "how can I help you?"

And it was then I was told that the promotion I had been offered was no longer available.

She said, "No longer available" as if some third party, a maleficent force, simply came down from the sky and stripped the position from existence. It was then I saw the coworker I hated most walk in, smiling, see the two of us standing together, become quite worried looking, and immediately turn around.

And I knew...

Oh, I knew!

The position was given to them. The laziest motherfucker I had ever had the sheer displeasure of ever knowing personally.

Left the office without a word: good riddance!

I texted my old dealer, hoping, maybe, he at least had some marijuana I could purchase.

He answered promptly.

I arrived at his house in what felt like moments, like, I had teleported there.

He opened the door, smiled, and said: "Hey—welcome back buddy!"

[IT WAS HERE A BLACK OUT FUGUE STATE ENSUED, OF WHICH NO COMMENT CAN BE MADE DUE TO THERE BEING NO EVIDENCE— THOUGH I SUSPECT SECURITY CAM FOOTAGE SOMEWHERE MIGHT HAVE SOME PROMISING LEADS]

And then I was back in my car, bleeding, covered in glass? Sweating? Having pissed myself?

And there was this ominous box in the backseat. I was so afraid of it. What it might contain. Until, of course, naturally, I had no choice but to look into the mysterious box.

Dilaudid, benzos, stimulants, LSD, marijuana, barbiturates… so many flavors of memory annihilators. Of pain extinguishers.

For a moment I thought of Tex. I thought of Kurt. Of the

promising ketamine, which, if administered properly, might absolve me of all the horrible moments that had come to ingrain themselves into my fucking brain these last two years.

I weighed my options.

Continue the binge.

Wait for my friends, for salvation.

DM to KKUURRTT: hey man actually, im good. no need to come bya

It is speculated, but not confirmed, that Cavin Gonzalez, following that DM to KKUURRTT, participated in the most horrific series of self destructive crimes one could possibly do unto themselves which culminated, unfortunately, in his gluing of a mop to both his head and ass, getting stark naked, and attempting to sneak onto a local farm by impersonating a horse. The farm which, he hypothesized, obviously housed an abundant supply of ketamine was extremely well guarded. Police were only able to offer this comment: "That farmer was well within his right to defend his property and his horses from that emaciated, tweaker ass loser."

An official autopsy was never published publicly.

Gonzalez's family attempted a wrongful death suit which was immediately rejected by the courts due to: "[THE DECEASED] being of such despicable character that, in fact, it was a righteous act to have [THE DECEASED] removed

from our plane of existence."

KURT

Decide to take the scenic route around the coastline, staring at the ocean instead of the road. Sure, I've got this on the other side of the country, but it feels different here. Like we've done something even if we haven't. Atlantic. Halfway past Panama City we get a DM from Cavin that reads: "not doing so hot, gotta take a raincheck guys." Take about ten minutes before I tell Tex what it says. There is an inherent strangeness in meeting up with someone you only know from the internet. Are they the person they really represent or just a brand putting words out there for the world to see, pulling wool just as Tex and I do? Tex's real name is Thomas and I do have a last name though not one to put in print.[7] We pull off for a rest stop and sit on the hood of the car trying to determine if we head back or push through. Knock on his door and shove spoonfuls up his nose saying something like "this will make you feel better," but less threatening. Check the stash and see that we're down past a gram anyways, not even enough to cure Cavin of depression like is being touted by every woke psychologist on the west coast. Fuck it. Keep going. All the way. Past Orlando and those great big theme parks that scream for our attention off the highway. Miami where we pick up Moondog and he takes us on his boat to the Florida

---

[7] KKUURRTT made me delete his actual last name a couple of chapters back.

Keys. Quick little detour to Cuba and then check out the Bermuda Triangle just to say we did. Is it us who return? We'll never know. Finish up the last of our drugs before we even got to share them. Guess this was why mailing them was a better choice than a road trip to a place we didn't even entirely know would be there.

After about an hour of sitting and watching the sun we head west again. Forget to film the end.

- TEXAS (AGAIN) -

AN ENDING

CUT TO:

We're back in East Texas. I had Kurt turn off I-10, take HW96 through Jasper, take HW69 north. Toward Sacul. Where my dad grew up. A good place to end—where things began at some point. I tell Kurt it's a shortcut but he knows it's not a shortcut. I've had the feeling again that this is the end—or at least an ending. I don't want to go back. I mean, I do. But I can't. There's something about this that tells me when I step out of the car the me that was in the car and the me that exists outside the car will no longer be able to exist together. Does that make sense? Probably not. But it's so hard to express that inexpressible feeling when you realize you've reached an ending.

There's an abandoned feed store up on the right. I recognize it. Not because I've been here, but it's from the dream. All of this is. Fields on the right. Woods on the left. Different, but I know this is the place.

TEX

Pull over.

KURT

Here? What is this?

He pulls into the weed-studded feed store parking lot—a cracked slab of pebbled concrete. Puts it in park.

> TEX
>
> I'm getting out.

This is where Neil Young's "Old Man" starts to play over the soundtrack.

> KURT
>
> Why?

> TEX
>
> I'm not going back.

> KURT
>
> Don't be an idiot. This is your car. What do you want me to do?

> TEX
>
> Give it to V. They'll need a car. I left some cash in the glove compartment. Use it for gas and all that —if you want. Or just leave it. A present V will find later. They deserve nice things and I... I just... What more can I do with all this? This is as good of a time and place to walk, you know?

I pull my bag out of the backseat. I don't know why. I won't need it. Maybe it's a comfort or something. Some attachment to hold onto as I near the permanent punctuation.

KURT

You're serious.

I don't say anything. He can see that I am.

KURT

You gonna be okay?

TEX

Maybe. Who knows.

I reach in the car, hold my hand out to him. He takes it—we shake for the first time in our friendship.

TEX

You know what's kinda fucked up but really funny?

KURT

What?

TEX

We never once stopped at a Cracker Barrel.

And then I salute him, shut the door, and turn away from the car. I never turn back. I hear the tires pop against the pebbles as he pulls away. House music starts to throb from inside the car. Music and tires on road growing distant.

There's a small dark figure moving toward me from the shoulder of the road I know leads to Sacul, Texas. It bounces on four legs. A black dog. I kneel down.

And this is where Neil Young's "Old Man" reaches it's chorus crescendo and where the camera pulls up and up and up, into the sky—the dog moving closer to me. The camera is high enough now so that my car driving away and me kneeling on the shoulder and the dog walking toward me are all visible. And up still. Faster, higher. Through the clouds. Toward the heavens. Through the shell that holds life to the earth. Out into the dark of space until the Earth is nothing more than a shape similar to the period at the end of this sentence.

IN THE MIDDLE OF NOWHERE
AN HOUR LATER

KURT: Where the fuck am I?

Open up Google Drive. Damn, I mean Google Maps.

This is where the end credits would go—white text as we follow this lone black dog walking along a country road in East Texas. "Old Man" would fade out and "Resignation" by Hans Zimmer & David Fleming would fade up. Blue sky, bright clouds. Quiet wind. As the song nears its end, the camera would hold and the dog would walk away from the camera until it's almost out of view and then everything would

FADE TO BLACK.

- POST CREDITS -

Bad Poet
@writtenwerd

○○○

If you guys need me to come up with something like "The End" or "To Be Continued" or "See You Fuckers Next Book" let me know - or use the above with a sarcastic "without Pete we would have never came up with this"

12:34 PM · Dec 18, 2020 · Twitter for iPhone

8

---

[8] No idea who this person is…

- APPENDIX -

TRANSLATION FROM PAGE 73

We enter Bucharest around eight at night. I pick up the package from the post office. It is small and stamped with many seals from the security department—both Romanian and American. I don't wait until I'm home to open it, so I open it in Krisztian's car. It's the book—a copy from *Heck, Texas* that I ordered from a private seller in America. Amazon won't ship the book here, so I had a Twitter friend named Dave buy a copy and mail it to me. I flip through it and see a picture of a woman with her ass on her face and poop on her nose. That makes me laugh. I show Krisztian and he laughs too. He starts the car and we return to the village.

Our village is small, but we have internet. There are buildings that were developed in the 1960s, but were never completed. On the top floor of the tallest building in our village—I made a small studio where Krisztian and I work. We write stories and screenplays. We are working on a TV show about an actor who wants to be famous and turns into a cartoon bunny. This is how we will become famous like Text Greshan and KKUURRTT. They are the most famous writers in our village. Everyone has a picture of them in their homes. We listen to their podcast ON THEE ROAD at night—even if it's just the one episode. They give us hope. Because if two careless men like Text and KKUURRTT can be loved by so many, then Krisztian and I can. Most of my face is missing. My father cut it with an ax one night while he was drunk. He thought I was his dead uncle and kept shouting, "You won't turn me back into wood, Geppetto!" I learned to live with half a face. I was born with a stomach on the outside of my body. Krisztian is not even human. It's a pig with a human brain. I hope one day I'll be as smart as him.

We are also big fans of Bud Smith. But we call him Butt Smith.

NOTES AND ERRATA

1.　Methamphetamine hydrochloride, a.k.a. crystal meth.

2.　Orin's never once darkened the door of any sort of therapy-professional, by the way, so his takes on his dreams are always generally pretty surface-level

3.　E.T.A. is laid out as a cardioid, with the four main inward-facing... No, that's not correct. I'm supposed to be talking about the car. Okay: and but so then they finally let me out of the trunk. I'd been in the trunk for like three, four, five days maybe, ever since Austin after the book signing, those two guys who didn't have a book for me to sign and who wanted me to go out back with them and "do a j" and since I haven't smoked marijuana in like ten years and I was in Austin and surprisingly they were the first to offer me reefer even though I'd been in the city for like two and half days and have been in the company of both men and women who looks as though their identity is shaped around the fact that they use marijuana daily—and because it is 100% legal in the state now, they can be totally open about that identity—and so when I take a short break from signing and join the two guys—who also look like their identity is shaped by the use of reefer (and maybe more than reefer, possibly a psychedelic or two)—they spring it upon me that they, in fact, do not have marijuana at all, that there is no "j" for us to do, and that what they want is for me to get into the trunk of their car as if I'm a hostage and this is a kidnapping for ransom, though they make no threat of such and just kindly ask me to get in the trunk, and since I am thoroughly bored with the signing and with my face cropping up in photo after photo and would, in fact, much rather be home with my dogs and my recliner and maybe the new Thomas Pynchon book, which I hear is a parody of *Infinite Jest* in a way that'll probably make me mad, and so when they say "Would you please get in the trunk and come with us?" I kindly oblige and climb into the trunk, which they have outfitted in a way that's similar to the capsule hotels in Japan—bed, TV, cooler with food and beverage, and a little funnel system that allows me to urinate and defecate through a hose that ejaculates out the side of the car as it travels at high speeds on the interstate—and the whole thing is rather comforting and before they slam the trunk they toss in a few books, including the new Thomas Pynchon book—which is titled *Hamlet Again*—and none of it makes me feel ill or fearful w/r/t my safety because they seem to have thought about it and seem to care about my well-being because, and this is pure conjecture, it seems like they care about my sanity and realized that I did not want to be at the signing anymore, playing the Author On Tour role—which I have never liked because it is so unnatural and against my neutral state of being, and so when they shut the trunk and I'm tucked in comfortably and when the tires start vibrating against the road, I find myself comforted, womblike, asleep in minutes, dreaming of being home, feeling like I am home, quietly forever overhead myself, dreaming and dreaming when I haven't dreamed in years, and this is how it goes for days—what feels like weeks, but when they finally let me out of the trunk I realize is only days, and by they I mean him because now there's not two guys but only one— and I'm okay being in the trunk this long, ignoring all the calls that go to my flip phone (because I refuse to own a "smart" phone), even though I know everyone thinks I've been kidnapped (because technically I have) and are wondering who they have to pay off (or find and kill) in order to get me back, and days later, in what looks like California—based on the palm trees and the piercing sunlight and the surf sound not far away—the trunk lid opens and one of the guys jumps back, surprised, screaming a little scream, and says something like "Holy shit I forgot you were back there"—a part of me is more than disappointed w/r/t my now having to leave the womb-like comfort of the trunk and return to a life that has grown predictably boring and stagnant, especially during the times that I am not writing but instead worrying about not writing or promoting the writing I've already done, but the guy tells me I have to get out of the trunk and offers to buy me an Uber to the airport—doesn't offer to give me a ride home, even though home couldn't be that far, given that this is clearly Southern California— and when I ask what happened to the other guy, this guy says something like "He's somewhere in Texas" and I nod because that's all I can manage and I take the Thomas Pynchon book because it is a parody of *Infinite Jest* and is in many ways so much better than *Infinite Jest* that I have to hate-read it many more times, and then the guy slams the trunk, cutting me off from my wombworld forever and says "Shit, man. Guess I'll see ya later" and then goes inside, into a small beach cabin which I'm assuming is his home, leaving me on this beach street, palms towering overhead, and before I can start in a direction toward the beach, I see someone across the street heading toward their car and stop them and they recoil from me like they probably usually do because they assume I'm homeless or drug addicted or a drug addicted homeless and they recoil further when I ask "Can I ride in your trunk?" and they hurry into their car and drive away, leaving me alone again, and so I head toward the sound of the surf crawling in and out and find a small beach that seems private, likely deserted because of the incoming army of dark clouds which creep inland from the sea like the high of a morphine drip and I sit in the sand and lay back, opening *Hamlet Again* again, starting at page one, reading this time for something deeper, some hidden message that maybe Pynchon has left for me to decode, and at some point I fall asleep, ease into a sleep that's nowhere near as comfortable as the trunk slumber but infinitely better on my legs because I'm able to stretch them out, and when I come back to, I'm still flat on my back on the beach in the freezing sand, and it's raining now out of a low sky, and the tide is way out.

About The Authors

KKUURRTT is glad you read his thing. He can be found on Twitter at @wwwkurtcom

TEX GRESHAM is the author of *Sunflower* and *Heck, Texas*. He's on Twitter as @thatsqueakypig and online at www.squeakypig.com